CLUBS

GAME OF GODS
BOOK TWO

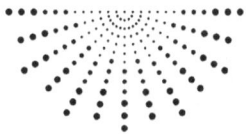

CHARLIE NOTTINGHAM

LIQUID MIND PUBLISHING

ALSO BY CHARLIE NOTTINGHAM

(Completed Trilogy—fantasy romance, more information on the origins of the Fae and Angels, how life began on earth, where Guardians came from, and—most importantly—a badass forbidden romance)

Origins

The Thrones of Ore and Ice

Creation

Sign up for Charlie's newsletter and receive a free copy of the Eluding Destiny prequel, Blood Bar:

https://liquidmind.media/eluding-destiny-prequel/

1
LATE MARCH, 2003

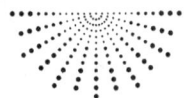

BROOKE

Fuck, the skill of this man.

Declan had me pinned to the wall, airborne aside from his hips pressed into mine. One of his hands was on my inner thigh, thumb on my clit while he kissed my neck.

His lips trailed down my chest, hooking around the button on my dress. Some people judged the ability of a man's tongue by whether they could tie a cherry stem with it. What about unbuttoning a shirt with it? Was that expert level?

He thrusted again, so deep that I had to bite my lip to keep from screaming.

"Don't hold back." He squeezed my hip, lips drifting to my nipple. He flicked his tongue a time or two. Then he bit me.

"Declan!"

He laughed, leaning back to meet my gaze. The hand that'd been on my hip came to my neck, thumb tugging my bottom lip downward as he applied just a *little* more pressure on my clit. "Brooke."

"That..." Another heavy sigh of pleasure, dropping my head against the concrete wall behind me.

"What's that?"

Almost unable to breathe, overwhelmed with the euphoria of his touch, the taste of whiskey from his tongue, I barely made out, "It hurt."

"But that little squeal was adorable." A kiss on my lips, this one softer than the last, despite his rhythmic thrusts quickening. "I love the noises you make. And you *love* that little touch of pain."

It was hard to argue when my legs were trembling, and it was taking every bit of willpower I had to keep from screaming.

But whether he liked it or not, I would continue swallowing those moans, no matter how badly they wanted to escape. Because behind Declan's head was a big glowing sign that read *Spades*.

We were in the bathroom of his bar. And sure, I adored a bit of exhibitionism here and there. But I didn't like the looks the middle-aged bikers gave me when I went back to the bar for a drink. And I *really* didn't like the fact that my moans were what those men would be thinking about when they went home.

"They can fantasize all they want," Declan whispered between kisses. "But I'm the only one who gets to touch."

I narrowed my gaze. "Stay out of my head."

He smiled, tucking some hair behind my ear. "If you keep trying to be quiet, I'm gonna *make* you scream."

In any other setting, I would've shot him a glare. But he acted on his threat before I had the chance, moving his fingers so much faster, thrusting in harder, bracing me against his chest when I collapsed forward.

There was no use in fighting it.

Burying my face into his neck, locking my arms around his strong shoulders, a deep moan muffled from my lips into his ear.

"There ya go," he murmured, moving my hair aside to kiss my neck. "Again."

Maybe I was masochistic, or maybe I was just playing into his game when I said, "Make me."

He stopped.

He stopped thrusting. He stopped kissing. He may have even stopped breathing.

Pulling back to meet my gaze, Declan arched a brow. "Excuse me?"

Yep. This was his game, and I was playing.

Fighting a smile, I said, "Make. Me."

He let out a half laugh and squinted me over. "And I was just about to say you were being such a good girl."

There was no denying the smile. It came to my lips, and it vanished just as quickly.

Before I realized what he was doing, my feet were on the floor. One of my heels gave out as he spun me around, pushing me against the porcelain sink. I tried to catch myself, but he grabbed my hands, twisted them behind me, and held them in place against my lower back. Just as the world stopped spinning, he fisted a hand in my hair and pushed it down, so I was only an inch or two from the mirror, able to see everything as he kicked my legs apart and plunged into me. He slammed against my G-spot with such force, such ferocity, that I couldn't help but scream.

"There." The hand in my hair released, coming to my clit. "I made you."

I smirked. Until he pounded in again, this time so hard that I edged forward, banging my forehead on the mirror. Not enough that I wanted him to stop.

Not once had I asked Declan to stop, come to think of it.

His fingers found my clit. I expected him to start massaging again, but he pinched his index finger and forefinger together.

I screamed, and not in a good way.

"And again," Declan said.

He went back to circling, which subdued the pain, filling me with pleasure instead. It rose and fell over me in waves, deep sighs easing from my lips, head rolling back with bliss.

"Are you gonna do as you're told?" he asked, octave deepening. His fingers spread out around my clit, and I knew he was going to do it again. "Or are you—"

"*Yes.*" It left me as a high-pitched squeal, finally submitting because I couldn't take it anymore. The game was fun, but only that. *Fun.* I wanted release. "Please don't stop."

He closed his fingers again, sliding them around my clit in that perfect rhythm he knew I loved. "Then behave."

I whimpered, bracing for his next thrust as the euphoria of his massage took hold. When it came, when he pounded deep within me, I let the moan fall just as it would have if we were on his couch or in my bed.

"There's my girl," he murmured, rewarding me with the freedom of my hands. Instead of letting them fall at my sides, he set one beside me. "Grab the sink."

I wasn't sure if my next moan was in anticipation or fear. But I did as I was told.

Just as I grabbed on, he thrusted in again. I screamed with bliss, meeting his gaze in the mirror as he bent forward for my face. Kissing my cheek, the hand that'd been pinning mine in place came to my neck. He squeezed, but not enough to cut off my air. Only tight enough to make it very clear who was ruling this scene.

The same one who always ruled the scene.

I'd tried to take charge, but it was useless. Never would a time come when I admitted I was a submissive person, but with Declan? Well, all he had to do was put his hand around my throat, tell me I was a good girl, and I'd do anything he told me to.

"Isn't it easier when you don't fight me?" he whispered in my ear.

"You love when I fight you."

He huffed. There was annoyance there, but also admittance. As if to say, *What fun would it be if you didn't?*

This was how things between us went. He pushed, I pulled. We fought, we bickered, then we did this until we were both lost in an orgasm-induced haze of euphoria, neither of us remembering why we'd been mad at each other in the first place.

It never really mattered anyway.

This was all that did.

Watching his face in the mirror, how beautiful his sepia skin sparkled when the sweat rolled down it, the hunger in those warm brown eyes, and their softness when they settled on me.

Fuck, I adored him.

Declan Caras had somehow taken over every part of my life in the last two years. He was who I thought of when I woke up in the mornings, who I fell asleep thinking about, and who I wanted to talk to when I read a new book I loved.

All that, combined with the fact that he fucked like a god...

"I'm gonna come," I moaned.

"Go ahead," he said in my ear, pulling my face up so I could see each kiss he gave my neck. "Be my good girl."

And there it was.

The explosion of bliss crashed through me, bringing chills to my skin, making my legs quiver. If Declan wasn't holding me upright, I would've fallen over. Everything blackened around the edges, blurring the rest of the room into nothingness. All I saw was Declan's crooked smile in the mirror as he maintained his pace, forcing me to absorb and get lost in every second of wonder my body could create.

Although, I wasn't sure if it was about my pleasure, or if it had far more to do with him getting what he wanted. After all, I was giving him the screams he'd insisted upon.

When the contractions finally slowed, he kissed my cheek. "Such a good girl when you wanna be."

I almost laughed, but he wasn't done, and the sensual grasp on my breast paired with his next intense pump into me was proof of it. No matter how hard he was going, how quick his pace had become, it somehow seemed softer than it'd been a moment ago.

That hand around my throat found my waist instead, holding me tightly around my curves. He didn't stop me when I reached around to touch his face, still watching him in the mirror as he watched me.

The expression he wore was always passion and desire until I finished. And then there was this. The moment when he transformed into the most tender, intimate lover.

I loved both, but this part... it was like aftercare before it was even over.

"Fuck," he groaned in my ear. "You feel so fucking good."

I gave him a moan in response.

Like his *good girl* always did the trick of bringing me over the edge, the right pitch to my moan and a hand in his loose brown curls always did the trick for him too.

His growl of pleasure vibrated into my ear as his warmth filled my core. When his breathing slowed, swaying hips doing the same, he spun me around, hooked his arms around my waist, and hugged me. A little too tight, but I wasn't complaining.

"God damn," he said through panting breaths. "What were we talking about?"

I laughed, resting my head on his chest. "I have no idea."

A deep sigh as he pulled his pants up his legs. "Shoulda written it down somewhere."

Smiling, I pulled away to button my shirt. "I'm sure it wasn't that import—"

"Hey, hey." He caught my hands, pulling them to my sides. "Not yet."

"What do you mean 'not yet?'"

"Give me five minutes. Then round two."

"How about round two tonight in your bed?" I finished buttoning my shirt and looped my arms around his neck. "At least then, you won't bang my head on the mirror."

"I didn't *bang* your head on the mirror." His hands found my hips, walking me backward to the sink. "I just kinda nudged it."

"Uh, no, you definitely banged it."

"I felt it. It wasn't that bad."

True, and true. It wasn't that bad, and he had felt it.

About two years ago, we'd met, we'd hooked up, and then our souls merged. Or they'd always been merged, and fucking activated them?

We weren't sure. All we knew was that we had fucked, and the next day, I felt him get shot. Then we could hear each other's thoughts, see out of each other's eyes, and hear out of each other's ears.

Declan referred to us as par animarum—Latin for paired souls. Apparently, they were an urban legend in the supernatural world, and we fit the criteria to call ourselves such.

"I'm sorry." He kissed me again, hoisting me up onto the sink.

"You don't sound sorry."

"Would it help if my tongue was between your thighs?" He smirked. "Because if that's what you need..."

"Are you fifteen?" I chuckled, pulling back to meet his gaze. "What's with you today?"

"I don't know." His smile was still wider than the sky, hands sliding up and down my torso. "I'm just in a good mood. And you smell amazing."

"Ah, that's what this is."

"What's what this is?"

"You wanna feed, so you're sucking up to me."

"Sweetheart, if I wanna feed, you let me feed."

That wasn't true. I'd told him no several times. He respected that. But nine times out of ten, he was right. I did let him feed on me. Not because he needed blood to survive. Keeping him from death wasn't a *bad* thing, but I'd be lying if I said I let a Werewolf feed on me because it was altruistic.

I did it because it was fucking orgasmic.

"No, I really don't know." He smiled still, eyes flicking over me. "Life's just good right now, ya know? And we've both been off two days in a row —that's nice. Rare, and nice." His palms drifted down my bodice. "And something about this dress and the way your ass looks in it."

I laughed. "You really are fifteen."

Grinning, he leaned in for another kiss, and then another, and another. Between them, he said, "Is that really a no on round two?"

I fastened my arms around his neck and tightened my legs around his waist. "If you weren't teasing me about your tongue between my thighs, my opinion can be swayed."

His lips curved higher against mine as he kissed again. This time, he traced slowly down my jaw to my neck. Flipping up my skirt, his free hand drifted up my thigh.

I shut my eyes, holding his shoulders and threading my fingers through his hair, as his kisses trailed down my body—

Knock-knock!

"Occupied," Declan called.

"Yeah, I'm aware," Emory said, voice low. He was the only other employee at Spades. Also Declan's best friend. "But you need to get the fuck out here."

"Is there a fire?" Declan was on his knees now, parting my thighs, and kissing the inside of one.

"No, but—"

"A fight?"

"No—"

"Then I couldn't give a shit less." Declan grabbed my hips and slid me to the edge of the sink.

"Declan—"

"Emory, it can wait—"

"*It's the cops.*" That sentence had all the aggression of a yell but the volume of a whisper.

Declan stopped. "What do they want?"

"I don't know, dude," Emory snapped. "You, I guess. They wanna talk to you. They wouldn't tell me shit."

Declan grumbled a curse as he stood. His shoulder slumped with disappointment, perhaps a bit of annoyance. "Rain check."

"I'm satisfied for the night." I smiled as I hopped from the counter. "Business first."

He sighed, leaned in for one more kiss, and zipped his pants. My heels clicked against the linoleum as we exited the bathroom.

Were cops at the bar uncommon? No. They'd shown a handful of times since I'd met Declan. Sometimes it was a traffic stop on the highway outside. Others it was a fight that got out of hand over a game of poker. But I'd never seen that look on Emory's face.

It wasn't concern, but fear shone in his brown eyes. Sweat dribbled along the line of his copper hair.

"What's the matter?" I asked.

"They said they were watching the back door," Emory said.

My brows furrowed in confusion. Because they thought Declan was gonna run? What from?

No, Declan wasn't known for his friendly demeanor, but he wasn't a criminal. He managed the bar, he went to the gym, and he fucked me. That was his life.

Declan was already walking through the stainless-steel swinging door by the time that registered. I took off in a semi jog behind him.

Three patrolmen, and one man in a suit.

Not a bar fight. Not a traffic stop.

"You own the place now, don't you, Declan?" the one in the suit asked.

"I do." Declan took a sip from his Jack and Coke from behind the bar. "What can I do for you?"

"Put your hands above your head," the man in the suit said.

Declan still held the glass. He glanced at it. "Mind if I put this down first?"

One patrolman reached to his hip. "Just keep your hands where we can see them."

Declan did so, not breaking eye contact for a second. Once his hands were in the air, he wiggled his fingers and gave a teasing smile. "I do have a pocketknife in my back pocket, but I'm not touching it."

"What's this about?" I asked, stepping forward. "He's been here all night. He—"

"Sweetheart," Declan said. "Please shut your mouth."

I didn't appreciate that, but it was spoken as softly as the 'sweetheart' at the beginning of the sentence.

One cop came around the bar and began patting him down.

"He didn't consent to being searched," Emory said, stepping up behind me. "He—"

"Do you consent to being searched?" the guy in the suit asked Declan.

"Well, he's doing it already." Declan's tone ranged closer to smart ass than his usual *shut up and leave me alone* attitude. "You gonna tell me what this is about yet?"

"Declan Caras, you're under arrest for the murder of Alicia Tanner—"

"What?!" I rushed forward, only for Emory to grab my arm and haul me backward.

The patrolman led Declan around the bar toward the exit. "Anything you say can and will be used against you in a court of law. You have the right to an..."

I spun to Emory and yanked my arm from his hold. "He didn't kill anyone. He—"

"Obviously," he snapped. "But we're gonna bail him out. We can't afford to post for both of you."

"Code to the safe is in the box under my bed," Declan called as they led him out the door.

And before you ask, his voice sounded in my mind, *I have no idea who Alicia Tanner is, and you know I don't fuck with drugs. But I have the right to remain silent, so I'm going to.*

CHAPTER TWO

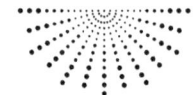

BROOKE

No sooner than they had hauled Declan out the front door did they line us up.

"Shut the fuck up," they'd told us. "Nobody says a word until we talk to each and every one of you."

"You either have to charge us or let us go," I snapped. "You can't just—"

"We found a dead girl behind this bar five minutes ago." A big cop around my height—around six feet tall—with the statue of a linebacker stepped closer, a feat I imagined intimidated the hell out of most.. On the younger side though, probably around thirty, with icy blue eyes and a firm set jaw.

I was never known for my petite stature. It helped that I was a Witch who could make this guy's eyes boil out of his skull with a few words under my breath, so that look didn't do what he thought it did. Or at least, not for the *reason* he thought it did.

"We can hold you all night, ma'am. So shut the fuck up and do as you're told."

"Who?" I asked, ignoring the fury ignited by the *do as you're told* comment. "Whose body?"

He was almost chest to chest with me now, eyes darkening with every heartbeat. "Did I not just tell you to shut the fuck—"

"My sister was supposed to be on her way here." I had no power in this situation, but somebody was going to tell me if the dead girl out there was my sister. "Ariana Lewis. Twenty-one years old. Long black hair, blue eyes, white skin. Is that who you found out there?"

Stiff shoulders loosening, the officer eased back a few steps. "She's blonde."

A deep breath of relief fell from my lips. Nodding, I stepped back and leaned against the bar beside Emory. Not to say I was happy somebody else was dead, but I was happy it wasn't Ria.

For the next three hours, they questioned us. They questioned Declan too, and a peek into his mind showed me the bullshit interrogation. They kept insisting he knew the girl. Declan kept saying that he hadn't, and the loop persisted.

The cops who interrogated us were less aggressive with their questioning. They showed us the dead girl's ID, Alicia Tanner, asked us if we knew her, if we had seen her inside the bar tonight, and we answered honestly.

Although I had spent most of the evening in the back with Declan, it didn't seem like she'd been here tonight. No one had seen her. Of course, the cops didn't tell me that. They wouldn't tell me anything. But they told Emory. Since they had arrested the owner of the bar, they had to refer to the bartender.

They were on to the last few of us, five people, when Emory and I finally got a moment alone to talk.

"I don't understand," I said. "How can they arrest Declan for murder when this literally just happened? Don't they have to build a case against someone to arrest them for murder?"

"They're supposed to." Emory grabbed a bottle of whiskey from the edge of the counter and poured two glasses. I assumed one was for me, but when I reached for it as he gulped down the first, he snatched it away, tilted his head back, and chugged it. "But they've been looking for a reason to throw Declan away since we were kids."

"The local cops just make a habit of framing toddlers then?"

He narrowed his gaze. "Hit the nail on the head."

This was how mine and Emory's relationship worked. He was Declan's best friend, so we spent a lot of time together, but we butted heads.

Emory was an asshole, and I was a bitch. We were both known for our sarcasm and lack of smiles. If not for Declan, I doubted we would've ever crossed paths, let alone been friends. Now though, after seeing one another almost daily, we loved to hate each other.

"Why? What's the beef here?" I asked. "Does it have something to do with his parents?"

"It has everything to do with his dad," Emory said. "Declan ever talk about his old man with you?"

More often than I talked about mine. "He's told me that he was in and out of jail and rehab for drugs, but that's about it."

"Not just drugs, but dealing. Trafficking. Murder, manslaughter, and a thousand other things. Only ever got charged with possession and dealing, though." Lowering his voice, Emory propped his elbows on the bar top and leaned in. "He had a lot of friends. Powerful friends. Guardians, Witches, Werewolves. You get the gist."

I was beginning to. Like there was an underground network of business in narcotics and gambling, there was an underground network of supernaturals in the human world. And those supernaturals had issues. The emotional damage from killing rogue Demons did a number on you. But some of us were just fucked up because of our shitty parents who had killed rogue supernaturals. And what happened to people like that?

Some of us left, like yours truly. Some of us ended up like Ariana. Barely an adult, addicted to substances to numb the horrors of our reality, but powerful as hell.

We were good at muling drugs, selling them, even killing for them, because we had paranormal abilities on our side. And the Chambers, the organization governing the underground world of supernaturals, did its fair share of killing, too. I had worked for them for a while to get myself through college. The money had been next to impossible to refuse. As a new adult, I had supported myself and Ria, trying to keep us both off the street and fed, and trying to keep Ria from returning to foster care. I'd made ends meet through part-time jobs, but had barely scraped by. Any hang-ups I'd had about the Chambers, about doing their dirty work, I put aside. In that line of work, killing for the Chambers, I had learned to be pretty damn good it. And at covering it up.

"Declan's dad was involved in the drug world, and they couldn't bust him for all the shit he was doing, but they knew he was doing it," I said.

"Yep.," Emory replied. "And Declan inherited that beef with the cops. The guy who'd pulled him down to the station, Detective Tyler, he's had it out for him forever. He knows there's something going on here. That it's more than just drugs, something supernatural. But he can't prove it. He's been trying to for years, almost lost his job over it a few times, but nothing ever sticks because there's never anything conclusive. Without substantial evidence in court, there's nothing he can do. But anytime something happens, whether it's a fight between a couple guys, or somebody putting in an anonymous tip about illegal gambling, this is what he does. Grabs Declan, brings him down to the station, makes his life hell for a few hours, then lets him go. It's never been anything this serious though. They might be able to hold him for a while."

"Or pin something on him that he didn't do ," I murmured. "Shit. You know any good lawyers?"

"Not off the top of my head, but we need to find someone from our world." He looked at all the cops scattered about our little paranormal haven. "And we gotta notify the Chambers. Possible exposure risk."

A valid concern that got my skin crawling.

It was unsettling. All the humans in this space. *Our* space.

There weren't many places like Spades. It was membership only. To become one, Declan sniffed you. If you were human, you didn't get a membership. Only people like us were allowed inside, and a guest if we could vouch for them.

By the rules of the Chambers, none of us were allowed to share our true identities with a human, but some did anyway. I never had. Never had enough friends to have to worry about disclosing that. But even so, when a human walked inside, we knew, and we were cautious. Exposure wouldn't end well for anyone.

"My connections aren't as deep as they used to be," I said, standing and walking around the bar. In my purse, I dug for my cell phone. Finding it, scanning through my contacts, I grabbed the landline off the wall. While I typed the number in, I said to Emory, "I'll find him one. And I'll meet them down there. Hopefully I can get him out by morning."

"You can't do that on your phone?" He gestured to the business line. "I'm waiting for your sister to call."

"I'm almost out of minutes. That little bitch has run my bill up so high, I'm gonna need to sell a kidney next month." As the dial tone sounded at my ear, I exhaled deeply. "You haven't heard from her at all?"

Again, he got closer and lowered his voice. "She was driving by when it was all going down. I guess she was carrying. Didn't want to come inside."

"Of course she was," I said under my breath. My knowledge of the underground drug world wasn't from research but lived experience. A lot of it I had gathered as a child when my dad was involved in it. But most of it, I had gathered from Ariana. My little sister who was actively addicted to heroin. "She say she'd call when she got home?"

"And that she was low on minutes, so she might just wait for you to get back."

Maybe I wouldn't have to sell a kidney after all.

"Hello, love." A voice with a heavy London accent came through on the third ring. "Depending, of course. Declan or Emory?"

"Brooke." Rolling my eyes, I leaned against the bar. "Sorry to disappoint you."

"And disappointed, I am." A heavy, almost taunting sigh. "But a call in the middle of the night, eh? That's never good."

Genevieve. I couldn't tell if I loved her or hated her. Maybe a bit of both. She never hid her affection for Declan, which was far from comforting. But she had helped us more than once in the year and a half we had known her. Not only was she a powerful Witch, but a connected one.

I didn't know exactly who those connections were. From what I could tell, she wasn't a part of the Chambers. Didn't seem to like them much either. But when I needed something, nine times out of ten, she came through.

"It isn't. Declan's in jail."

"*What?*"

I explained, ending with, "You know any good lawyers?"

"Jesus Christ," she grunted. "Aye, I know a few. What's your budget like?"

"Ideally, no more than two hundred an hour."

"And if you need to post bail?"

With a deep breath, I rubbed down the bridge of my nose. "I'll put my house up if I have to." Declan would do the same for me. "Of all the people I've thought I might have to do that for, Declan wasn't on the list."

"In our world, darling, everybody should be on the list."

"Oh, I expect a lot of the people I care about to end up in jail at some point. I'm just not willing to post bail for most of them."

"I know what that's like." Genevieve laughed. "I've got to ask though, darling. Did he do it?"

First of all, I wouldn't have admitted to it over the phone if he had. Second of all? "Of course he didn't do it. You think we go around offing random people, Genevieve? Just for the fun of it?"

"Well, I've seen wolves kill for less."

"Less than the fun of it?"

"*Far* less, love."

"Well, Declan isn't one of those wolves," I snapped. "Can you give me the number or not?"

"Quite testy for a woman begging for help."

"It's almost 4 AM and I'm exhausted. Apologies."

She must've sensed my sarcasm, because she said, "I can tell. I'm looking for the number now. Ah, here it is. Ashley Montgomery." Genevieve listed off the number, and then said, "Give her a call. She'll want extra for waking up so early."

Looked like I might be selling that kidney after all. "Great. Thank you."

"Mhmm." I had just lifted the phone from my ear to put it on the receiver when Genevieve said, "Wait."

Sighing, I brought the phone back to my ear. "Yes?"

"Have you remembered anything else?" Her voice was softer now. Hopeful. "Anything at all?"

One more deep breath.

About a year ago, images had started flashing through my mind. At first, they were blurry, like a TV whose antenna needed adjusted. Gradually, they had become more vivid.

Running through a snow-blanketed forest. Chasing after a black wolf the same size as me. Tackling it to the ground, rolling with it through the snow, biting at each other's faces and scruffs. Because yes, I'd had one of those.

At first, I cracked them up to sweet nothings. Odd fantasies. Then they grew more realistic. So realistic that, at times, they felt more real than my own flesh. So much so that it scared me. I'd gone to Genevieve and asked what she thought it meant. She'd chuckled and said that more than likely, in the life where I had met Declan, he wasn't the only Werewolf in the relationship.

Since then, more memories had come through. Flashes of a man who wasn't much of a man at all, but a boy in his late teens. To me, he had seemed a lot like a man. And he looked a lot like the one I called my boyfriend now. Beautiful brown eyes, warm brown skin, and a crooked smile.

But I didn't only see Declan—or whatever his name was then—in those flashes. I saw others. Women whom I called friends. Women whose names I didn't know. All I remembered vividly was my time with them, the way they made me feel. Feeling for them the same way that I felt for Ariana. A sisterhood that apparently spanned hundreds, maybe thousands of years.

I remembered my home as well. It was always snowy. Snowier than any place I'd been before, and that was saying something for a girl born and raised in Oregon. All the foliage was black for some reason. That stuck out.

But if Genevieve was asking if I remembered a clear story or life, the answer was no. I remembered being the girl whose memories were floating back to me, but I didn't remember her story, nor the romance with the man she'd found again in the modern world.

"Bits and pieces," I said. "It's all patchy. Why?"

"Curiosity. I know it kills the cat and all, but I just wanted to know. What about Declan?"

"Not that I know of."

"Interesting." With that tone, I could envision her face. Brows pinching together, head slightly tilted. Absolutely fascinated. "I wonder why that is. He's clearly the one more invested in your relationship, and yet you're the one who remembers—"

"Alright, fuck off."

Her laugh sounded through the speaker as I set it onto the receiver. As soon as it stopped, I picked it up again and typed in the numbers she had given me. Ashley answered on the third ring. Apparently she lived close, only about fifteen minutes from the precinct. Spades was about half an hour away, so I told her she would beat me there. She said that was fine, so long as I brought my checkbook.

Setting the phone down, I flapped my lips together in a trill.

"You got him a lawyer?" Emory asked.

"Yep. Heading there as soon as I can leave here." Scanning the room, I counted two people still lined up for questioning. "Am I supposed to wait?"

"They told us to hold off until they talk to everybody." Emory nodded to a cop at the door. A cute guy on the heavier side with brown hair and brown eyes. If not for the fact that he was a cop, and the fact that I was taken, I would've done him. "I saw that one checking out your ass, though.

I bet he'll let you go if you bat your eyelashes right. And unbutton your top."

Grumbling, I did so. "Don't tell Declan. Last thing we need is him killing a cop while he's under investigation for murder."

Emory snorted a laugh at that, the closest the two of us got to bonding. "My lips are sealed."

As I found myself doing so often tonight, I took one more deep breath. Then, I put my assets to work.

CHAPTER THREE

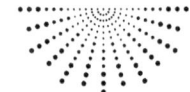

DECLAN

Suspicion of murder.

I had been arrested for *suspicion* of murder. On the car ride here, through the metal grate, I had asked, "So who did I kill again?"

Detective Grant Tyler had clarified then that they'd only arrested me under the pretense of *suspicion* of murder. I thanked him for the explanation and smart mouthed for the following twenty minutes to the local police station.

That's where I was now. Sitting at a metal table, on a metal chair, looking at a mirrored window. I smelled and heard four people on the other side. One was Tyler, and the other three—two more men and one woman—I didn't recognize.

The room was cold and grey, no furniture besides the metal chairs and table I was cuffed to. The fluorescent lights were harsh, and seemed to flicker at just the right frequency to make detainees develop headaches. The first few minutes I was left alone seemed to stretch for hours, but I knew it couldn't have been that long.

I had been in rooms like this before, never for anything this serious, so it wasn't entirely unfamiliar. I knew the boredom and discomfort was supposed to get to me, supposed to feed my nerves. But I couldn't say I was surprised by any of this. Detective Tyler and I went way back. Or rather, Detective Tyler and *my father* went way back. As much as I loved my dad, and as much as I hated that he was dead, he was a dick, and the cops had plenty of reasons to hate him. He had something of a motorcycle club, which dismantled upon his death. They hadn't been known for being upstanding citizens though, and Dad was the worst of them all.

He'd had a drinking problem, gambling problem, and the occasional drug problem. With addiction came chaos. There were frequent fights at his bar—now my bar, Spades—which resulted in regular visits from the authorities. Tacked onto the typical bullshit that came with the clientele of a biker bar, Dad had dabbled in the sale of illegal substances. Everything from weed to heroin at some point or another. That's what'd landed him in jail several times when I was growing up.

Mom took over Spades when Dad died, and although some shit had caused problems over the years, Spades was calmer than it'd been. Drugs weren't my thing, so when I'd taken over, the place remained stable. But it was a bar, a supernatural bar at that. So yeah. Shit happened on occasion.

And every time something did, Detective Tyler was there, waiting for the day he could hit me with all the charges he'd never been able to stick on my dad.

I had no doubt that's what was happening here. There had been a dozen cops around the back of my bar when they'd loaded me into the car. That must've been where they'd found a body. I owned the place, so I was the first suspect. Or, at least, that was how they were spinning it.

I didn't know whose body it was, or why it was there, but I had nothing to do with it. Was I a killer? Sure. I was a Werewolf, and shit happened. But I hadn't killed anyone lately. I would never kill a woman, either. Whoever they had found, it didn't have shit to do with me.

Door hinges squealed to my right. Walking into the interrogation room, Tyler nodded to my cuffs. "Those too tight?"

"Can't complain." I leaned back in my seat. Once he was in his, I stifled a yawn. "Look, I don't know what you found, but I didn't do it."

"Pretty sure a body found outside your bar's got something to do with you."

Confirmed my suspicions. "When was this?"

"Got an anonymous tip about an hour ago." Tyler propped his elbows on the table, leaning in with narrowed blue eyes. "They said to look at the dumpster behind Spades. So we did. And sure enough, there's a body there."

Cocking my head to the side, I choked on a laugh. "And you think I did it?"

"I think you're the first person I should look at."

"Why would I kill someone and dump them behind my own bar?"

"I don't know. Why'd your daddy kill Harry Thompson in that same parking lot fifteen years ago?"

According to Mom, he'd tried to rip Dad off on an ounce of blow. "Don't think he was ever convicted of that."

"But we both know he did it."

"Hey, your word's better than mine. What was I when that happened? Ten?"

"Something like that." Tyler leaned in closer. "That's the cycle, isn't it? Kid sees his daddy killing people, selling drugs, so when he grows up, what does he do?"

"Well, I don't sell drugs, and have yet to commit a murder, so the apple must've fallen pretty far from the tree," I said. "We both know I didn't do this. Ask your questions and let me go."

Tyler glared at me and sighed. Then, after reaching into his briefcase and pulling out a folder, Tyler slid a photo across the table. A pretty girl. Blonde hair, brown eyes, pale skin. Not someone I recognized. "You know who this is?"

"I can say with absolute certainty that I do not. But basic deduction skills tell me this is probably the girl you found behind my bar."

Clenching his jaw, Tyler ran a hand down his beard. "And that's your response? No remorse?"

"Jesus Christ. Look, if she's dead, I feel bad for whoever's missing her. But no, I don't feel remorseful, because I didn't fucking kill her. I don't even recognize her."

"So she has never been into your bar?"

That, I couldn't say with certainty. I knew she wasn't a member. The members, I all knew by name and by face. This girl? She wasn't ringing any bells.

But that didn't mean that she had never been inside. It was possible somebody else had escorted her. If I had her smell, I could confirm whether she had been there while I had been there. Smells, I rarely forgot. Those stuck out clearer in my mind than physical appearances.

But I knew enough about this line of work to see what he was doing. He wanted me to trip. He wanted me to say that she had never been in my bar, then show me proof that she had been. "Not that I can clearly remember. But I can check my guest book. She'd be in it if she'd been inside at any point."

"You gonna make me get a warrant for that?"

I opened my mouth to speak, but the door swung open again. "We absolutely will."

A woman in her early forties entered the room, wearing a black jacket and slacks with a white button up underneath. Her hair was in a slicked back ponytail, blonde waves descending to the middle of her spine. She wore a thin dusting of makeup, but nothing fancy, with a pair of glasses. She looked sharp, if a little tired.

"Ashley Montgomery. I'm Declan's attorney, and he will now execute his right to remain silent." She took the empty metal seat beside me. "So, let's get this over with, shall we?"

Tyler looked at her, then at me, and laughed. "Only guilty men lawyer up this fast."

"Or smart men." Ashley relaxed in her seat and pushed her glasses up the bridge of her nose. "Especially in a case like this. One where the cops have an obvious vendetta against someone who's never committed a crime."

Tracing his tongue along his teeth, Tyler gave a witty, sarcastic half-smile. "Let me grab you something to drink, Miss Montgomery. I'll be back in a moment."

Once he was out of sight, and the door shut behind him, Ashley turned to me. "You say nothing. And you sit the hell back. Stop giving him those 'I'm the alpha' eyes. You're going to get your smart ass thrown in jail if you don't swallow your pride and shut the hell up."

Fair enough. My mouth had gotten me in trouble more than once. I lifted my thumb and forefinger before my lips and twisted, as if turning a key.

"Good." She turned back to the table, then set her eyes on the photo. "You don't recognize her?"

I shook my head.

Ashley nodded. "Good. That's good. As long as you have nothing to do with this, we'll get this thrown out."

"Did Emory call you?"

"I didn't catch her name. Saw her outside though. Pretty redhead?"

Huh. Brooke. I wished I could say I wasn't surprised, but I had a hard time figuring out how, exactly, Brooke felt about me. She wasn't on the list of people I would count on bailing me out or finding me a lawyer in the middle of the night. But she had come through for me after all.

***

After a few long hours, they wound up letting me go. And who was waiting in the parking lot? The pretty redhead who'd gotten me the attorney. Apparently, she'd already paid the fee, because as soon as we walked outside, Ashley told me she wasn't concerned about me going away for this. as long as no evidence was attached to me. Just to get used to saying, "I want to speak with my lawyer."

As I thanked her and said my goodbyes, Brooke rounded the corner in a sprint. There were very few times had I seen Brooke sprint, especially with a smile like that. When she practically leaped into me, heat gathered in my chest.

Wrapping my arms around her waist, I whispered into her ear, "Thank you."

She kissed my cheek. "You would've done the same for me."

I would have, but that wasn't the point.

A lot of the time, it was hard to tell if Brooke cared about me at all. She was the center of every one of my days. And she'd said I was the center of hers, but I was never sure how much I believed that. How much I *could* believe that.

We were going on a year and a half now. We saw one another everyday. Took trips to the nearby forests. Read books on the couch together. Cuddled, and watched movies, and fucked each other's brains out.

That all sounded so sweet. Like a rom-com. But it had taken nine months before she let me call her my girlfriend, and me, her boyfriend. More days ended in fights than not. But they usually lead to some great makeup sex, or hate sex, so I had to count my blessings there.

For a moment, as she pulled back, took my face in her hands, and looked between my eyes, it felt like we were really in this together. Like she cared as much about me as I did about her. "What happened? Are you okay?"

"I'll be better once I get some nicotine." I nodded to the car. "I've got a pack in the glove box, right?"

There went the loving look in her eyes.

This was a frequent fight. She hated that I smoked. But I guessed she figured I deserved a cigarette after having spent my night in jail because she nodded and said, "You can smoke while we drive. Let's just get out of here."

Smirking as she walked around the car to the driver's side, I grabbed the handle. "You must've really missed me."

"Or"—she shot me a glare, lowering herself to the driver's seat—"I just really hate this place."

"You missed me." My smirk worked into a smile as I sat beside her. "You would make me smoke outside if you didn't."

Still glaring, she rolled down the passenger window. "You're going to exhale every bit of that smoke outside of my car."

"Yes, ma'am."

She heard my mocking tone and raised with a dramatic sigh. Shifting the car into drive and pulling into the roadway, she said, "You didn't do this, right?"

There went my smile. "Yeah. Because I had time to kill some random girl while I was balls deep in your pussy."

"I'm just making sure."

"You think I just go around killing people, Brooke?"

"Neither of us are known pacifists." She shot me a look, somewhere between annoyed and disappointed. As if I should've known she meant no harm. "I'm literally just checking. You don't need to get defensive."

Like she wouldn't be defensive if I accused her of murder after spending four hours in an interrogation room. But she was right. This time, at least.

Lighting the cigarette, I took in a deep breath that gradually loosened my tight muscles and allowed me to relax into the cool spring breeze floating in from the open window. "I'm sorry. It's been a long night."

"It's okay." Brooke's eyes were gentle when they met mine before returning to the road. "But what happened? Do they have anything on you?"

"Not a damn thing." I explained what had gone down, touched on why they'd seen this is the perfect opportunity to arrest me, and ended with, "I don't know what happens next. But I know they'll breathe down my neck until they find someone to hang for this."

"Alicia Tanner," Brooke murmured. "It sounds familiar, but just in passing. She's not a member, is she?"

Shaking my head, I breathed in another hit. "Definitely not. Last name doesn't ring any bells for me. I don't even know if she was human."

"Maybe I'll go to the library and do some digging. You want to come with? Or you want me to drop you off at the house?"

Brooke was simply thinking of my well-being without raising an argument. A rare occurrence.

"You need some sleep too, ya know."

"I'll sleep when I'm dead." She rolled her window down. "Which is probably gonna be soon with all this secondhand smoke you're blowing at me."

I held my arm further out the window. "There's literally no way it's blowing at you."

"Well, it is." Veering to the right, she merged into the turning lane. "And I don't understand. Somebody kills this girl there, then calls the cops. Why would they do that?"

"Somebody who's pissed at me? The cops trying to frame me? Hell if I know."

"Yeah, but you haven't had any beef with the cops recently, have you?"

The most recent visit I'd had from the police was two months ago. A couple guys got into a fight. I told them to take it outside, they did, and it got bloody. Somebody driving by must've called it in. But that was a quick, *hi, bye* situation. "Not that I can think of. And it's not like I'm involved in anything shady. Nobody has good reason to frame me. Especially for murder."

"Whoever it is, they must be stupid. If they wanted to set you up for murder, they should have built a better case. Given you a reason to kill someone, then fabricate evidence of the act."

I snorted.

Glancing from the road to me, she smiled. "What?"

"You say that like you have experience."

She tried to pull her smile down, unsuccessfully, and kept her gaze on the road. "What can I say. I worked for the Chambers."

"You framed people for murder?"

"It's a long story."

I laughed. "You did. You framed innocent people for murder."

"Calm down, I did not frame *people*. I just framed one person."

"That makes it a lot better."

"Don't take that judgmental tone with me, mister. He'd already committed murder. Cops couldn't prove it, and neither could I without exposure. He was some rich, untouchable son of a bitch. I couldn't get my hands on him, so I set him up." She paused, looking my way again. "Don't repeat this."

"Never. But I have to know the story."

"Keep blowing that smoke at me, and you're gonna live it."

"Jesus fucking Christ." I pinched the cherry off the cigarette and stowed the remaining butt into my pocket. "That was just something you casually did when you were working with the Chambers. Murder."

"Don't say it like that." She frowned at me. "I'm not a psychopath. There was a job that needed doing, and I did it."

"I'm not saying you're a psychopath. Just that it's fucked up. That they made you do it, I mean."

The slow release of her shoulders told me how much that meant to her. It was a weight she carried, apparently, and it was nice for someone to acknowledge that. She'd only been a teenager when she'd started working for them. No one had thanked her for that, nor acknowledged the damage it'd done.

Of course, I *assumed* that was what her reaction meant. I didn't know much about Brooke. Sure, we could read each other's minds, but we'd agreed long ago that it was an invasion of privacy to do that regularly. As a person, I knew her well. But her life story was a mystery. All I did know? Her father was in prison, her mother had left when she was young, and then she'd gone on to work for the Chambers in college.

Her emotions were no different. Anything I learned about the way Brooke felt was guesswork. The release of her shoulders, a half-smile, the glint of a tear she wouldn't let me see. This was all I had to go on.

I loved her more than I loved just about anything. But fuck, I hated that this was the closest I got to her letting me in. I could read her mind at any time, but communication? Knowing how she felt? I knew when she was pissed, and that was about it.

"It is what it is," Brooke said. "But don't get high and mighty here. I'm not the only murderer in the car."

"I have killed four people and only because I had to."

"I didn't have a choice either. If I had, I still would've chosen to kill them."

She *shouldn't* have had to. But that was a conversation for a different time. A time when I had the patience to coax it out of her.

"So what do we do now?" Brooke asked. "What if they try and pin it on you either way?"

"I put up the house for a good attorney," I said. "When we get back, let me run to the safe. I'll pay you back for Ashley."

"I'm not worried about it. Just get a shower and relax. Then meet me at the library, and we can talk about whatever I figure out. You should probably do some digging too. Maybe ask regulars if anybody knew this girl? I know her name from somewhere."

"That's nice of you, sweetheart, but I'm paying you back."

"It's really not a big deal—"

"It is." My voice came out firmer than I'd intended. So firm that she shot me a glare more volatile than I had seen her give in a long time. Which was saying something for how often we argued. "I don't want you to pay for this. You didn't do anything. I'll handle it."

"You didn't do anything either. And I already gave her the check." Brows furrowed, she huffed. "This doesn't have to be a big thing."

"But this is a big thing. So just wait for me to run inside and grab the money—"

"Why? Why is every single thing a fight with you, Declan?"

"How is me wanting to pay you back for my lawyer starting a fight?"

"Your attitude is what's starting a fight. I don't care about the money. I care that you're being a dick for no reason."

"If you didn't care about the money, then you wouldn't care about me giving it back to you."

"Jesus fucking Christ. Is this some"—she altered her voice to sound like a caveman—"*I man, you woman,* things? Because God forbid I pay for dinner, right?" Again, she lowered her voice. Sounded just like her caveman imitation. "'It's a man thing, Brooke. People see me letting my girl pay for our dinner, and they think I'm a shitty boyfriend. Don't put me in that position, meh, meh, meh.'"

"I don't sound like that."

"That is exactly how an emasculated man sounds."

"You call me a dick, and that's all well and good, but you don't think it makes you a bitch to find pleasure in emasculating your boyfriend?"

"I think when he's being an insecure caveman, he could use a little emasculating."

"I think if I said that about you, you'd throw a bitch fit."

"Alright, you know what." She jarred the car into the right lane so fast, I bonked my head on the panel between the front and back seats. Slamming the car into park, she unlocked the car doors. "You wanna see me be a bitch, here we go. Get out."

Laughing, I shook my head. "Drive the car, Brooke."

"Little old me?" This time, it was a southern bell impersonation. "I'm just a silly woman. I don't think I can, sir."

"This isn't because you're a woman—"

"No, it's because I'm a bitch." Her tone was playful, smile no different. But there was the slightest pinch in her raised brows that said she was, in fact, pissed. "So go on. Get out of my car."

"You're seriously gonna make me walk."

"It's been such a long night. Fresh air might do you some good." Reaching past me, she fumbled for the door handle. When it clicked open, she gestured to the open field. "We're only a few minutes from Spades. Ten-minute walk. You can handle it."

I snorted again. She kept smiling. "C'mon, Brooke. Drive the damn car."

"I'm such a bitch. And this is what a bitch would do." Again, she gestured outside. "She'd also expect an apology once her grumpy ass boyfriend has gotten the stench of jail off his clothes and a nice nap."

"You're dead serious right now, huh?"

"As a doornail."

I held her gaze a moment longer before realizing just how serious she was. She was annoyed, not mad. But I'd gone toe to toe with the bull, and bulls didn't bluff.

Laughing again, unsure if I was annoyed or aroused, I unbuckled my seatbelt. "I'll remember this."

"I bet you will."

I got out of the car and slammed the door shut. I propped my arms on the open window and glared at her inside. Glared, but smiled. Cars whooshed past, making the cool air whip around me as they flew by. "I'll remember it the next time you're begging me to let you come."

"Just make sure you call me a bitch then, too." She smiled and glared as well. "At least degrade me when I can get off on it."

"It's gonna be a while before I let you get off again."

"Mm, guess I'll have to find someone else to help with that."

"You do that, sweetheart, and I'll let you keep the money." Smirking, I backed away from the car. "'Cause you'll have to use every cent of mine to get me out of jail."

"I don't make idle threats, baby." She shifted the car into drive, sparing me one more smirk as she merged onto the quiet morning road. "As you can see."

"I see you regretting this later," I called.

She flipped me off in the rearview.

And I laughed.

Maybe this was why we fought so much. Not because we hated each other, but because, for us, it was foreplay.

CHAPTER FOUR

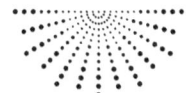

BROOKE

He was the light of my life, he really was, but I couldn't stand him ninety percent of the time. I wasn't ashamed of that. I was one hundred percent certain he felt the same way about me.

Our relationship wasn't normal, and I couldn't call it healthy, but I loved it. It worked for us.

After abandoning my wonderful, pain in the ass of a boyfriend on the side of the road, I continued to the library. My shift didn't start for another two hours, and it wasn't ideal to show up in the same clothes I'd worn to work yesterday, but I had a routine for this. In the trunk of my car, I kept a *stayed up way too late, drinking way too much, getting fucked all night,* go bag. Others kept a spare pair of sweats, a few hoodies, and a blanket in the trunk so they were prepared to get stuck in an Oregon snow storm. My bag was more fun.

So when I got to work, I locked the door behind me, changed into a work appropriate sundress, and brewed a pot of coffee in the breakroom. It was a slow day with only a few patrons milling about the library. I knew I could hole up and get some research done without getting bothered. Java in hand, I sat at my desk and got to work.

Alicia Tanner. Who was she?

The internet answered that question a hell of a lot quicker than I expected.

Despite her common name, narrowing the search results by location brought up court dockets and mug shots, all for the same person. Two years ago, she was arrested for possession of heroin. A year ago, arrested for theft. Two months after that, arrested for theft again.

I hated to say it, but I wasn't surprised that she'd wound up dead. Not because she deserved it. No one deserved to die like she did, let alone get discarded behind a bar like a piece of trash. But the sad reality was a brutal life of crime often led to just as brutal a death.

It was a horrible fact. One I'd seen play out a dozen times over throughout the course of my life. Moreso, throughout my childhood. Then all over again when I'd worked for the Chambers.

I had mostly killed Demons and rogue Vampires under the Chamber's guidance. People like Alicia weren't my usual targets, but when I got a case they *were* the usual victims. If a Vampire wanted to drink someone dry, who better than a criminal? Someone society wouldn't miss. Rogue supernaturals tried to keep the heat of human authorities off their ass. Killing a CEO or politician's kid would be like putting a glowing red target on their backs. But who'd miss a dead thief or addict?

That said, given the fact that her body was found behind a supernatural biker bar, I had to wonder if the two were correlated. Had she died because of her connection to the drug world? Did it have something to do with the same world Declan's dad had been a part of? The details I had gathered about Declan's dad were vague. But they were vivid enough that I knew a dead body in a dumpster wouldn't have been completely out of place in the life he had led. The problem was, he was long dead.

Before Declan had taken over running Spades, his mom had run the bar for years. Was it possible for something, someone, from those days to have held out this long? The cops certainly thought so. But their vendetta against Declan and Spades seemed baseless these days.

Or was she connected to the bar some other way? If she wasn't a member, as Declan claimed, was she killed by someone who was? It had something to do with Spades, that much was undisputable. But the question was: how? Why?

Was it about Declan? It must've been. If it had just been about a drug deal gone wrong, they wouldn't have put in an anonymous tip. Perpetrators reporting their crimes were damn near unheard of.

Those involved in a life of crime, however, were known for their anonymous tips. One dealer, or runner, or mule, would turn in another to flush out their competition. Declan wasn't competition, though. As far as I knew, he kept his nose clean.

If not for our history, I may have doubted the likelihood of that. *Maybe I don't know him as well as I think I do*, I would've thought. *Maybe he has a whole other life I don't know about.*

My instinct to paranoia, to assume the worst, lost out here. I knew Declan like the back of my hand.

Raging pain in the ass or not, his involvement in this world stopped at the bar. In the year and a half that we'd been together, he'd taken one hit off a joint. He drank, often in copious quantities, but in fairness, he got the same buzz from ten beers as I got from one vodka cranberry. It took a *lot* for a Werewolf to get fucked up.

In fact, I'd been fucked up more frequently than he had since we'd met. Once. That was how many times I'd gotten drunk since we started dating. Not once had I seen Declan drunk. Tipsy enough to get stupid twice. But not drunk. The man owned a bar, and I'd never seen him get past tipsy.

So, despite my instinct to turn to paranoia, I knew that wasn't the case here.

He wasn't dealing, either. Sure, he made an okay living, but my librarian salary paid better. The difference in our incomes was something I knew he was insecure about, hence our fight this morning.

But that wasn't the point. Someone dropped a body behind his business and immediately turned it in. Meaning someone was pissed. Someone was setting him up.

I couldn't find much more about Alicia online, but her name was a gateway. In the phonebook, I found her address. It was about fifteen minutes from the library, ten minutes from my place, going the same direction. Not a wonderful area, which wasn't surprising given her arrest record, but that was a good thing for me. Neighborhoods like that—like mine—didn't ask questions. But the neighbors were always peeking out of their blinds.

Since my shift ended at 2 PM today, that was next on the list. Jefferson Heights. I knew the area well because when I was in college, I lived one street over.

That apartment had been one of my favorites. Aside from the mice.

The mice were gross. But the apartment was cheap, and I liked the city view out my bedroom window.

It looked the same as I remembered it. A four story, red brick building. More apartments sat on the left and right, most of them taller and at least a little newer. It made the building look short and wide, like it had been squished into place. All of the windows were the same, uniform and framed in white trim. Some were adorned with tinfoil as makeshift curtains. The building had a glass entryway, only accessible with a key code.

Across the street were townhomes. With porches. Porches with swings and chairs, where a few women huddled together, gazing out at the quiet road.

If I'd learned anything working for the Chambers investigating and solving crimes, it was that older women sitting on their porches knew *everything*. Their neighbor's work schedules. What every kid on the block did for fun. How many people lived in their house. Where they went. Who was a frequent guest.

So I couldn't say I was surprised when I exited the car, and two of those women squinted at me, speaking quietly amongst themselves. Doing my best to give a friendly smile, I started toward them. The one on the right— a Black woman wearing a pretty floral bonnet—bounced a baby on her knee. She returned the smile, but said something I couldn't catch to the woman who sat beside her—a white woman, likely approaching seventy, wearing a blue housecoat that looked like something straight out of the sixties.

I wasn't able to tell if I was welcome or not, but I tried my best to sound friendly when I said, "Hey there."

The two women were sitting across from each other on wicker furniture, floral print cushions peeking out from behind them. The porch was neat, and obviously a spot in frequent use. A broom rested in one corner, and there wasn't a single dead leaf or speck of dirt to be seen on the porch or its narrow stairs. A few potted plants sat along the railings. A wrought iron fence kept the world out of the small, lightly manicured yard that laid between me and the porch.

"Well, hello." The older one glanced between me and my car. "You meeting somebody, hon?"

"Not exactly." Clutching two posts of the wrought iron fence, I leaned in to see them better. "I was actually hoping to talk to you. Or any of the other neighbors, I guess. I'm looking into a murder that took place last night."

"Yeah?" The younger lady readjusted the baby when he fussed. "You with the cops? Because they already talked to us, and we don't know anything."

They already knew about Alicia. That made this easier. "No, not with the cops. But... Well, I think the cops might be trying to pin this on a friend of mine." Saying boyfriend would've been more accurate, but it also would've made me sound a lot more biased. "He never even met her. So I'm just looking into things. Seeing if I can figure something out that they can't."

Slowing her bounces of the baby, she cocked her head to the side. "And you are...?"

"Brooke Lewis." Giving another smile, I stretched a hand over the railing.

"Well, we can't reach you down there." The first woman laughed, and the second joined in. "Go on through the gate. Come have a seat."

And so, I did. I made my way up to the porch, and sat on a wicker chair across from Maya—the older white woman—and Beatrice—the younger Black woman. Maya insisted on getting me a coffee. I'd already had five today, what would one more hurt? I'd been up all night, and I could feel my focus starting to slip as the adrenaline wore off. Plus, I wasn't about to argue.

Maya brought me a teal mug from inside. The coffee was hot, and smelled deliciously rich. I could stomach the sixth-cup-jitters for anything this good. Just the first sip had me feeling more alert again.

"She's a good girl." Gazing down at the child in her arms, Beatrice let out a slow, shaking breath. "Was, I guess. A good mama too. She might've had a needle in her arm on the regular, but these babies had everything they needed and more than they wanted." She pinched his chubby thigh, then tickled his nose until he giggled. "High or not, she took care of these babies."

A knot formed in my stomach when I looked at that little boy. This was always the part where I got attached. It was just a case until I saw the family. "He's hers?"

"Yes, ma'am." Maya nodded inside. "Her toddler's taking a nap on the couch."

Jesus. Mother of two, murdered and dumped behind a bar.

"I'm so sorry for your loss," I murmured, looking between them. With frowns and deep breaths, they nodded their thanks. "Were you all close then?"

"Close enough, but not great friends," Maya said.

"We just look out for each other around here," Beatrice said. "She got some funding through the state to pay a sitter. It ain't much, but she didn't trust sending them out to one of those welfare daycares overnight. And that's when she worked, so."

Couldn't blame Alicia there. Although I'd never gone to a state run daycare, I'd been to state run foster homes growing up, and I'd never let a kid I loved go into one of those. "What did she do?"

"Well, her taxes would say she's a waitress," Beatrice said.

"But that was her daylight job. And she took the kids with her there," Maya said. "It's the night job she needed a sitter for."

Which could've meant a lot of things. "What's her night job?"

"Lady of the night, if you know what I mean," Beatrice said. "We think, at least. Don't know anything for sure."

Damn. This was hitting a hell of a lot closer to home all of a sudden. My sister was also a "lady of the night," a sex worker. Every time she left the house, I was terrified that she wouldn't make it home. Last night, Alicia left her babies with Maya and Beatrice. She didn't make it home. Would *never* make it home. I had spent so many nights worrying over Ria meeting a similar fate.

Their shared profession could be a good thing, though. Ria might be able to tell me more about Alicia. There was a good chance that between their work and the drugs, their paths had crossed. Maybe they at least knew *of* each other, if nothing else.

"Do you know if she worked with anyone?" I asked. "Other girls?"

"I know she left with a man a lot," Maya said. "He never got out of the car, so I don't know what he looked like. Can't tell you his name either. But he drove something nice."

"BMW, I think," Beatrice agreed. "Had those wheels inside the wheels that spin? I don't know what the hell they're called."

Neither did I, but I knew what she was talking about. "Sure. Sure, I gotcha. You never even got a glance at him though?"

"Not clear enough to give to a sketch artist," Beatrice said. "Saw him hanging his arm out the window smoking a cigar though. Always had a damn cigar. Not those cheap ones from the gas station, either. Smelled pretty damn good, actually. Definitely white. Could be anywhere between thirty and sixty."

"That helps a lot," I murmured. "Thanks for all this. The coffee, filling me in. I appreciate it."

"Thanks for looking into it," Beatrice said. "Somebody needs to get justice for that girl. She didn't deserve to die like that."

"No one does," I said.

"Doesn't sound like your friend, huh?" Maya asked. "You still don't think it was him?"

White guy, BMW, fancy cigars. That was all valuable information. And none of which could be used to describe Declan. The ethnicity could be misconstrued to describe Declan. In the winter, when his skin was lighter, he passed as white. But he was biracial, and none of the other details fit him. He preferred cigarettes to cigars, and there was no denying his choice of vehicle. You wouldn't catch him dead in a BMW.

"No, definitely not. And I was with him at the time of her death, so I know he didn't do it." After a sip of my coffee, I exhaled deeply. "But the cops have it out for him."

Maya snorted. "They never did it, and it's always the cops just hating 'em."

Beatrice laughed. I couldn't help laughing myself. I knew the point they were making.

"Look, if he hadn't been with me, I'd look his way too. But he *was* with me."

"Alright, alright." Maya held up a hand in surrender. "If you say so."

"Anything else we can help you with?" Standing and resting the baby on her hip, Beatrice gestured inside. "I gotta get these two ready to meet their aunt. She's next of kin, so it's on her from here. A nice girl. Young, but better off than Alicia was."

I was happy to hear that. My next question would've been, *Where do the kids go now?* "One other thing, actually. Do you, by chance, have a key to Alicia's apartment? I was just hoping to take a look around. That can help in situations like this."

Maya chuckled. "You a little detective?"

Well, there hadn't been a job title for what I did for the Chambers, but in essence? Yes, that's exactly what I'd been. "Just a concerned citizen."

"Yeah, I got a key. I'm going there to pack their bags up," Beatrice said.

"As long as you don't take nothing, I'll let you on in."

Good. Because key or no key, I would've gotten into that apartment.

The apartment was cute. Basic, but cute. Like most apartments, the walls were a boring shade of beige, but Alicia had decorated with nice stock prints. A few oil paintings hung on the walls as well. They were old, likely purchased at thrift stores or flea markets, but they brought some color and life into the space.

The kitchen was nothing special. Just a galley with enough room to throw a couple meals together. The dining area was about the same. A basic table in the center of the room, a few mismatched chairs scattered about. The place was lived in, with toys and things of that nature sitting around, all of the chaos of having two young children, but overall it was well-kept and clean.

The living room was the most notable space. Instead of a standard sofa, there was a pullout bed in the center. No coffee table, but two bedside tables, a small dresser beneath the window on the right, and a wardrobe beside it that was doing its best to act as a room divider separating the dining space from this one. It was minimally decorated, a few nicknacks on the dresser, a couple of framed pictures of her kids. The bed was made.

"CPS requires kids of different genders to have their own rooms," Beatrice had explained on her way down the hall. "Alicia made this her bedroom so they'd each have their own."

Beatrice disappeared down the hall, leaving me to look around. I wasn't sure what I was looking for, but any information I could get was worth my time.

Sitting on Alicia's bed, I opened the bedside table. Inside were the basics. Bras, socks, panties. Nothing special.

I continued to the other side of the bed. In those drawers, nothing notable either. Some clothes and lingerie. Same for the dresser.

The wardrobe by the window, however, was exactly what I was looking for. A quick peek inside told me everything I needed to know.

Candles. Shiny crystals. Daggers with intricate designs and gems embedded into the handles. At the center of it all sat a leather-bound book. There were no words strewn across it, but it didn't need a title. I had one just like it tucked in a wardrobe of my own at home.

This was Alicia's book of shadows. Alicia Tanner was a Witch.

CHAPTER FIVE

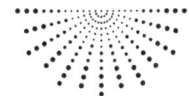

BROOKE

"Oh, hey." Standing in my living room, wearing my shirt—might I add—Ria propped her hands on her hips. "I didn't think you'd be home yet. I thought you got off at seven today."

No, that was on Mondays. It was Saturday. And work was the last thing on my mind.

I dropped my duffel to the hardwoods and all but jumped across the room to her. Tossing my arms around her shoulders, breathing in the smell of cigarette smoke and alcohol, I exhaled with relief. Not because of the cigarettes and alcohol, but because she was here. She was okay. It wasn't out of place for her to disappear for a night or two, or for her to flake on our plans. But it wasn't every day that someone in the same line of work as my sister was found dead behind my boyfriend's bar. "Thank God you're okay."

Ria laughed. "Of course I'm okay." Sliding her hand up and down my back, she squeezed me tight. "And I get a hug and everything? Just for being okay? I could get used to this."

I rolled my eyes but it was fair. I wasn't a particularly affectionate person, not with anyone. Declan and Ria being the exceptions. Ria was my baby sister, and I had taken care of her our entire lives. She saw a softer part of me that I kept hidden from almost everyone else. But even that softness only extended so far. I just wasn't a touchy-feely, sweet-hearted person. And I definitely wasn't much of a hugger.

Pulling back, I patted her all over. Like I was examining her for an injury. "Where the hell were you last night?"

"With a client," she said, cocking her head to the side. "Why?"

A better question was: why was her nose running, her eyes bloodshot, her skin clammy, and her pupils their normal size? Normal here *wasn't* normal. Pinpricks, that was normal for Ria.

"If you were with a client last night, why are you going through withdrawals right now?"

Stepping back, she let out a huff. "And here I was thinking you'd be proud."

"Are you getting clean? No more drugs for you?" I arched a brow. "In that case, yeah. Very proud. But I don't think you're getting clean. I think you're just out of drugs and I'm wondering why."

This time, it was more of a sigh than a huff. "Dude was a runner. He left with my money. I tried to chase him, twisted my ankle in the process, and I am *pissed*. But I got another job tonight, so." She shrugged, rolling her eyes. "Not the point. I'm fine. What happened? I don't think I said that I was coming to Spades for sure, anyway."

Fair. She hadn't. She said she *might* come by Spades.

"Somebody dumped a body behind the bar."

Ria's jaw fell open. "What?"

"Alicia Tanner." Lowering myself to the couch, I patted the seat beside me. "Did you know her?"

"Fuck if I know. Why would I know her?" Ria sat beside me. "And why the hell didn't you guys just cover it up? You could've done that, right?"

Things only people in our family said. "Because we didn't find the body. Somebody called it in. Anonymously."

Eyes widening, she shook her head in confusion. "That doesn't make any sense."

"Preaching to the choir," I said, scooting back into my corner of the couch to better face her. "It's gotta be somebody trying to frame Declan. That's all that makes sense. But Declan doesn't have enemies. Yeah, I'm sure he's pissed some people off at the bar, but not enough for this. It just doesn't make sense. And you know what else does doesn't make sense?"

"What's that?"

"She was a Witch. She was one of us," I said. "And you and her are in the same line of work. That's why thought the two of you might know each other."

"Stripping?"

"Sex work," I said. "She's got a few charges for solicitation, possession of narcotics, and a couple for assault."

"How the hell'd you learn all this?" Ria swatted some snot from her nose with the corner of her sleeve. Or rather, *my* sleeve. Since it was my sweater and all. Doubted I'd be wearing that again anytime soon. "Did you talk to the cops?"

"Not really, but they talked to Declan. Spent hours questioning him. They know they don't have a case. But the body got dumped at his bar. She was beaten to death—that's what one of the cops said—so it couldn't have happened there. Someone would've heard it." Massaging my eyes, I collapsed my head against the cushions behind me. "You're sure you don't know her?"

"I don't know a Alicia Tanner. If you had a picture or her street name, I might recognize her. But otherwise..." She trailed off with a shrug. Then, despite her sickly appearance, she managed to smile. "Mine's Bubbles."

"Bubbles?"

"Bubbles. There's a story behind it, but I don't know if you want to hear it."

I grimaced. "I think I can live without knowing."

"Suit yourself." She stood again, this time pacing the room. "Where does she live? I'm assuming that's how you found out she's a Witch, right? You went through her shit?"

"Jefferson Heights," I said. "Can you sit the fuck down? Your pacing is making me nervous."

"Well, I have restless legs right now, so suck it up." Flipping me the middle finger, she grabbed an open can of ginger ale off the TV stand. After a sip, she stifled a yawn. "I do know a couple people out there. But you're not giving me much to go off here with her real name and no picture. Give me a picture and I can ask around."

It was a bit of a Hail Mary either way. "I'll print out a picture of her at library tomorrow. Will you be here to pick it up?"

"Probably," she said. "I get off at five, so I can come here when I'm done. Or I can meet you at the library."

"Library works better," I said. "Just, please, don't forget. These cops already have beef with Declan. They're trying to find any way they can to pin this on him. I know he didn't do it. I need to make sure he doesn't go away for it. If he does, I'm breaking his ass out and we're running to Mexico."

"How about Canada?" Ria asked. "I don't think I'd tolerate that heat well. You are taking me with you, I'm assuming."

I smiled. "Wouldn't have it any other way, you little pain in the ass."

Laughing, she set her ginger ale back onto the TV stand. "You love me."

"You're *lucky* I love you."

Again, she flipped me off. And again, I smiled.

In the two years we had known each other, there had been a few times Declan had asked why I put up with Ria's antics. More than once, I'd given her money, or gotten her clothes, or whatever else it was she needed, even if it meant I went without. I'd complain about how high my phone bill was, or that I had to dip into my savings to pay the electricity, and he'd say, "Why do you keep helping her then?"

I'd always copped an attitude. "Why's it your business?"

He'd back off, but I had started dissecting that question. Why *did* I keep helping her?

She was my sister, sure. But she was my best friend. My only friend outside of Declan.

It had been me and Ria against the world my whole life. Yeah, she was high more often than she wasn't. But she had a kinder heart than I did, and I liked who I was with her. I liked that her kind nature encouraged me to do the same.

Ria's expression changed, the joy leaving her eyes. "You don't think they can charge Declan for this, do you? There are witnesses and everything, right? He was with you last night. He didn't do it."

Biting my lip, I raised a shoulder. "I hope not. But we both know how cops are. They could plant evidence to make it look like it was Declan. Hard evidence matters a hell of a lot more than eyewitness testimony. Especially if they don't have anyone but me to vouch for him."

A hard swallow bobbed her throat. "I'll ask around."

Behind me, out the bay window that crested the couch, the rumble of a motorcycle approached. I only knew one guy who would be in my driveway with a motorcycle. "Speak of the devil."

"I have a meeting with a client in a couple hours," Ria said. "But you know how you said you loved me?"

I shot her a look. "Uh-huh."

She gave me a sad, sweet smile. "Well, do you love me enough to loan me some cash? Or even to give me those Vicodin you got from your dental work a couple years ago? I know you have them hidden in here somewhere."

I frowned. "I can't give you drugs, Ria."

"I just need something to get me through the session with my client. He's a good guy. I know he won't run. All he really wants to do his bitch about his wife and kids anyway."

My moral qualms with that statement didn't make me feel much better about giving her drugs or money. But that was too big of a conversation to tackle right now.

"I can pay you back in the morning. Even in Vicodin, if that's what you want."

Another deep breath escaped me.

"I'm sorry. I know you hate when I do this, but I just feel like shit." Tears welled in her eyes. "I've been sick all day, and I just need a little bit to get me through."

At least she was asking. Very easily, she could've gone into my purse and taken the money. I preferred she asked rather than stole.

It was the last thing I wanted to do, but I couldn't think of a better alternative. I went to my purse, snatched a fifty from my wallet, and handed it over.

I could've sat there and thought. Thought about how I was enabling her. About how this money would cause her more harm than good. But what did it matter? She was going to get high tonight either way. I would rather she didn't do anything desperate or drastic to get drug money in the meantime. Giving her this felt like I was mitigating some risk, at least.

I didn't like it. Hated it, actually. But my baby sister was sick. And she asked for it so sweetly. So I gave it to her. Just like I always did.

CHAPTER SIX

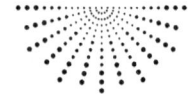

DECLAN

As much as I wished I could say I was angry at Brooke for kicking me out of the car, I wasn't. Not in the slightest. The run was needed. It was only a few minutes from Spades and the highway cut through a densely wooded area, so I ran through the trees in wolf form. It wasn't exactly a difficult feat. As soon as I entered a clearing away from civilization, I stepped out of my clothes and tied them around my ankle. I didn't encounter any furry creatures that would've made for a good snack along the way, but I had fed off Brooke last night anyway, so I wasn't exactly starving.

Brooke, though, I wouldn't have minded taking another bite out of.

But the fact of the matter was, she was right. I was a dick. But she was getting that money back, whether she liked it or not. And no, it wasn't a "I man, you woman," thing. But I would explain all of that to her later.

Now that I was home, my priority was getting the smell of prison off of me, grabbing something to eat, and figuring out who the hell Alicia Tanner was. But that would have to wait, too, because when I walked inside, I was greeted by a familiar face who never would've kicked me out of his car.

"What the hell happened?" Emory asked from his perch on my kitchen counter. Glancing past me, he furrowed his brows. "Where's Brooke? I thought she was picking you up."

Snorting, I dropped my shirt and boxers onto the couch, having only put my jeans on when I stepped out of the woods. "Oh," I said, "she did. She picked me up, and then she made me walk home."

He laughed. "Start at the beginning, please."

So, I did, ending with, "I was being an ass. I can't blame her."

"And she was being a bitch. Seems like that's the way you guys work. No offense, man, but you and your girl fighting is at the bottom of my priority list right now."

Touché. "Yeah, me too, I guess. Do you know that name? Alicia Tanner?"

Emory joined me in the living room. Scooting back on the armchair across from me, he shook his head. "No, doesn't ring any bells. We know most of the members by name."

"And she's not one, I know. Why the hell was she dumped behind my bar, then?"

"Beats the hell outta me." Running his fingers through his beard, he gazed off in the distance in deep thought. "Maybe the Chambers have something to do with this. Are you up-to-date on your taxes and everything?"

"If there's one thing I never miss, it's my taxes," I said. "Even if I had, that wouldn't make any sense. The Chambers protect their secrecy at all costs. If I had ripped them off, I'd be dead. They wouldn't have framed me." I paused. "Well, Brooke said that she framed somebody when she worked for the Chambers, so I guess it's possible, but I still can't see it. He was a killer the Chambers were trying to hunt down. I'm obviously not."

"Clearly," Emory said. "I'm guessing Brooke is digging into this? She must have some resources at the library, plus whatever sources she has from when she was still working for those pricks."

"That was the plan, until I pissed her off."

"You've pissed her off many times before, and I'm sure you're gonna piss her off a thousand more times. She's still looking."

"Probably," I said under my breath, pausing again. "Alright, I know I was a dick. But it was more my tone than what I said, right? Wanting to pay her back, that's just basic decency. That's not controlling, is it?"

"Fuck if I know," Emory said. "Brooke is a puzzle I'm never gonna put together. If she weren't your soulmate I would've told you to leave a long time ago. You love the hell out of her, and I don't think she even likes you."

It was me who snorted this time. "You and me both," I murmured. "No, I know she loves me. She just got some fucking issues. She needs therapy. That's the problem."

"Are you sure about that?" Emory asked. "Because I don't think I've ever heard her say 'I love you.' She says it every time she gets off the phone with Ria—every time Ria leaves the room—but I don't think she has ever told you 'I love you.' Not in front of me, anyway."

"Yeah, she has. Just yesterday, she said 'I love you.' I told her 'I love you' before I left to run over to the store. And she said 'I love you, too.'"

"No, she said, 'you too.' That's not really the same as 'I love you.'"

Cocking my head to the side, I thought back on it. She *had* said "you too." When I told her I loved her for the first time, she had said "I feel the same way." She didn't say I love you back. And now that I thought about it, I couldn't think of one time when she had said the whole phrase.

"You've never heard her say 'I love you' to me?" I asked.

"Not once," Emory said. "Ria and I had a bet going about when you'd realize. Another one for how long it would take her to say it."

Slouching, I let out a dramatic sigh. "Not once."

"Probably not the time to bring this up. Go get your shower, man. We'll do some digging and see if we can figure out how Alicia is connected to the bar when you're done."

———

I tried to think about something else while I showered, but that was *all* I could think about. Not once in almost two years had Brooke told me that she loved me. Now that I thought about it, I remembered her saying "you too." An occasional "mhmm," an "I know," but not a single "I love you."

Why? Why say "you too," and "mhmm," and all the other combinations without the actual word? Was there a story there? Or was it simply her inability to open up?

The latter, I imagined. No matter how hard I tried, she just wouldn't open up. She loved stability, normalcy, humanity—I knew that. I had learned it in one of our very few deep conversations.

Very drunk, we'd been talking about society. I mentioned that when I was a kid, I had wished there was a school for people like us. I had hated feeling like the outlier for being a part of the supernatural world. She said the opposite. When she was a child, she had wished she was human. Not because she hated having powers, but because maybe she would've had had parents who stuck around. Parents who were responsible, who loved her as much as she loved them.

That last bit, I had always inferred. It was too vulnerable for Brooke to admit aloud. That girl avoided vulnerability like the plague.

There was too much going on at the moment to address it directly with her, but I wanted to confirm my suspicions. She was already pissed at me, so I couldn't expect much, but I would tell her I loved her when I saw her tonight, just to make sure that I wasn't making this up. Or rather, that Emory wasn't.

When I got out of the shower, Emory suggested I get some sleep. That wasn't happening. Sleep felt impossible. Instead, we went over to Spades. I pulled out every club member book going back twenty years.

Emory was already seated in the booth with some paperwork strewn out before him. It was barely noon, so probably not the most responsible time to start drinking, but a bad day was a bad day. Whiskey in hand, spilling it along the way, I grunted a curse.

As I stood back up to grab the bottle, Emory lifted a fifth of Jack Daniels from the seat beside him. "One step ahead of you, unless you're gonna be picky."

"Not today." I snatched the bottle. Twisting off the cap and lifting it to my lips, since apparently, I wasn't capable of keeping a glass upright at the moment, I glared at the stack of paperwork on the old mahogany tabletop. "No Alicia, huh?"

"Not yet, no," Emory said. "You don't have a picture of the girl by chance, do you?"

"They showed me one at the police department, but no. I don't have one on me. Why?"

"I can ask around about her." Whooshing some auburn hair from his face, Emory eyed the documents. "I'll know if anyone's lying to me. Or rather, they won't be able to."

Ah, yes. One of Emory's most prominent and important abilities. He could do lots of things—Angels could—but his most useful ability was one I didn't have a name for. He made people tell the truth. Not through intimidation, not with violence, but simply by looking at them the right way.

I'd asked him how it worked once. He had used it on me a few times growing up, but when I had finally asked, he said he didn't understand the question. "What do you mean, 'how does it work?' It just works."

According to him, all he had to do was look at someone and want them to tell the truth, and they had no choice but to.

It was a cool trick. Useful, I guess. I preferred getting to turn into a wolf.

"I'll see if I can get a picture from the cops. If not, I'm sure Brooke can print one out at the library." After taking another swig of whiskey, I stood and started to the safe below the bar. I didn't keep money in there, that stayed in the back, but it was where I kept the rosters of the guests the members brought with them.

"They said she was bludgeoned to death. Why the hell would anyone bludgeon a woman to death?"

"Incite fear?" Emory asked, crossing his arms against his chest. "Maybe even to scare you."

"And what am I supposed to be scared of?" Continuing back to the booth with the book in hand, I laughed. "Some pussy who beats women? I'd kill that fucker in a heartbeat and not lose a second of sleep over it. If this was supposed to scare me, all he did was piss me off. And if it's about trying to send a message, don't you think they would've done it in smarter way? Like, I don't know, let me know who the fuck they are?"

"You'd think," Emory said. "But I've got this strange idea that whoever this bastard is, he's not very intelligent. Would have known better than to fuck with you if he were. Or, I should say, he would've known better than to fuck with Brooke Lewis's boyfriend. She's the one they should worry about."

Laughing, I flipped open the most recent guestbook. It spanned from late last year until now. Starting on the first page, I scanned each name for a Alicia, or a Tanner, but wasn't surprised when she didn't show. "You don't really believe that, do you?"

"That Brooke would kill for you? Oh yeah, I believe the hell out of that."

"And you still think she doesn't love me?"

Letting out a deep breath, Emory raised a shoulder. "She can't stand me, but she would kill for me. Then make my eyes melt out of their sockets or some shit just for inconveniencing her, but I have no doubt that she'd kill for me."

I wasn't sure what point he was making. Was it that Brooke just didn't show love the way that the rest of us did? Or that she was just fucked up? Or that she was a psychopath who maybe enjoyed solving cases and killing people a little bit too much?

I didn't know. I doubted anyone did. If anyone had ever seen the softer side of Brooke Lewis, I would've loved to sit down and pick their brains. Because even though I could go inside hers at any given moment, I never had any idea what was going on in it.

———

After dotting all my Is, crossing all my Ts, flicking over every name in the guest book for the last two years, which was a shit ton of fucking names, I found nothing. Many Alices, a number of Alicias, but no Alicia Tanner. I made note of each one though, then tabbed it with a Post-It note to come back to. Maybe Alicia Tanner was a married name, and her maiden name was somewhere in my records.

What I needed to do was get my hands on something of Alicia's. If I smelled some of her belongings, I might recognize her scent. While I didn't remember everything I saw, it was rare for me to forget someone's scent. It was how I remembered most things. It was a much stronger sense, and I relied on it the most. It had yet to fail me, while my eyes often did me a solid disservice.

Either way, by the time I was done going through all the paperwork, it was approaching four. That meant that Brooke would be getting off work and I could go make my amends. Might have to sell my dignity in order to do so, but it was a price I was willing to pay So that was what I did. Headed to her place.

Shutting off the engine of my bike as I rolled into Brooke's driveway, I noted Ria's van parked across the street. I couldn't say me and Ria were close. We weren't best friends by any means, although she had become my best friend's good friend. But she was a sweet kid. And Brooke loved her.

Reaching into my saddlebag, I lifted out all of the necessities. They were a little squished, but I knew Brooke wouldn't mind. With a brown bag in hand, and some semi-squashed flowers tucked under my arm, I started up the cement walkway. Brooke was already opening the door by the time I reached the threshold. Hands on her hips, lips pursed, she said, "You smashed them."

"Just a little. The ones in the middle are fine. Just gotta pick out the ones on the edges."

She glared. "Fuck you."

"I mean, if that's how you want to make up—"

"I don't want to make up." She snatched the bag of Chinese from my hand and the flowers from under my arm. "I want an apology, and then I want you to get back on your bike, drive your ass home, and come back with flowers that aren't ruined. Then we can talk about making up."

"You really want me to go get you new flowers?" Smirking, I shook my head. "It's not happening."

"Then have a nice night." She snapped the door shut, but I caught it before she could click it into the lock. Struggling, pushing with all her might, to no avail, she glared at me through the half a foot gap. "Fuck you. Let go of my door."

"I'm sorry. I was a dick this morning, and I'm sorry. You had every right to make me walk. I shouldn't have talked to you like that."

Her glare softening, she did her best to hide a half-smile. "I don't know if you're forgiven yet, but I believe you enough to open the door." Pulling it closer so there was more air and less wood between us, she wagged a finger. "But that's not an invitation inside. You don't get that until you just accept that I'm giving you the money, and there's no—"

"I'm not going to take the money, Brooke."

"Jesus Christ—"

"But not for the reason you think," I said quickly, hoping she wouldn't snap the door in my face before I could finish. "My dad was a piece of shit. I loved him, I really did. But he was a piece of shit. And every day—or at least, it seemed like every day—he was in trouble. He was either nodding off at dinner, or pulled over for a DUI, or getting Spades raided for trafficking, or dealing, or whatever the crime of the week might have been. My mom filed bankruptcy trying to save his ass. She paid lawyer fees to keep him out of jail more times than I can count. And I don't wanna be that guy. I don't want my girl to pay for my fuck ups."

Expression softening, Brooke's tight shoulders released. "But it's not—"

"My fuck up, I know. I didn't do this. But it felt too similar. And I don't want to do that to you. I love you too much for that. I don't want to be a burden in your life. I just want to make it better. It was bad enough you had to come pick me up, but I have to pay my own lawyer fees. Please."

She frowned, then nodded. "Alright. I understand that. And I appreciate it, even. But you could've said that instead of calling me a bitch."

"I'm sorry for that too," I said. "I love you. I love you a whole hell of a lot. And I promise I won't call you a bitch again."

Letting out a deep breath, she gestured inside. "You better. And you better not."

There it was again. Anything but, "I love you." In this case it made sense, but I would try again later once the fire had burned out some more.

Throughout the evening, we caught up on what information the other had gathered. Unfortunately, according to Brooke's research, Alicia had never married, so she certainly wasn't in my records.

But Brooke let me pay her back, and we talked on the couch, and we watched some TV, and we ate the Chinese food, and she accepted the crumpled flowers, and we laughed, and we smiled, and we fell asleep in each other's arms, cozy in her bed.

While I dozed, I remembered why—despite the bickering, despite the drama—we were here. Because holding her was the most comfortable place I'd ever been. Hearing her breath, filling my lungs with the scent of her hair, feeling each pump of her heart against my skin, was the best place in the world. The best place in *any* world. I knew we were fucked up. Both of us. I had my issues—mainly my attitude—and she had hers.

I wasn't with her because she was my soulmate. I hadn't *fallen* for her because she was my soulmate. Whatever the fuck that even meant. I chose her. Every day, every bicker, even when she made me walk home, I chose her. Because something about us just made sense. Something about her, about me and her, just felt right. Maybe it had more to do with that soul-mate thing than we realized. But maybe it didn't.

Maybe I liked that she never said I love you. Maybe I liked that she was damaged.

Such a stupid word. As if she was broken.

She wasn't. Maybe she had been once, but she had put herself back together. Maybe all of this, her attitude and the way it clashed with mine, was why I loved her. Maybe I loved all the reasons I hated her. She was cold, distant, but when she was curled against my chest, she was the warmest place I'd ever been.

Maybe it was the friction. I loved that she was strong, determined, that she didn't put up with my shit. I would've loved her if she even more if she would put her walls down for me every once in a while. But fucking hell, I loved that those strong walls protected her from everything. Even if she still feared I was someone she had to protect her heart from.

CHAPTER SEVEN

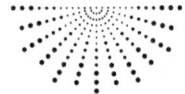

BROOKE

Cool wind bit through the fabric of my clothes, but the heat of his body pressed against mine was the perfect counterbalance. Something hard, rough, scraped against my back, even through my clothes. With every gentle rock of his hips against mine, it scratched, but I didn't mind.

Didn't mind in the slightest.

As his lips traveled down my jaw, I rolled my head back. It was only then that I realized I was pinned against a tree. That's what was scraping my back. Its bark. A pine tree, to be exact. A pine tree with black needles. At first, I thought they were green, and it was only the dark night that distorted their color, but that couldn't be so. After all, the light coming from the moon wasn't its usual blue. It was red.

Finding it among the stars, gazing up at it as he kissed my neck, making me gasp, I stared up at those twinkling lights in wonder.

Everything about this moment felt electric already, almost as if there was some imaginary energy budding between us that no one else could feel, no one else could see.

I knew what love was. I'd felt it before. But I had never felt this before, not even in my current life.

The warmth of his body, the tenderness of his touch, and all the passion that held it together was unlike anything. Nothing compared to this. Not even Declan, and I wasn't sure why that was.

As his lips trailed further south, so did his fingers. They skimmed down the back of my thighs, making me gasp. That gasp only intensified, morphing into a moan, when he hoisted me around his waist and peeled back the fabric of my shirt to reach my breast. His lips circled around my nipple, only teasing at first, then moving faster and faster.

Never in my life had I felt something like this. So intense, so warm, so soothing. Maybe an awkward word choice given the situation, but that was the only word I could think of. It didn't feel rough, violent. It was erotic and arousing, of course, but somehow safe.

At least, to her, it was.

This wasn't a dream. The blue planet framed in yellow rings that came into view when I coiled further back was proof of that.

I'd seen that before in another memory. In that one, though, I was running, and my heart was racing, and I was so afraid. So afraid, until the man before me, the same one who was licking my nipple now, had stopped me with his wall of his chest, only to yank me into a nearby bush.

I still didn't understand that memory. I wondered if I ever would. This one, though, I understood completely. It was our first time. That's why it felt so intense. It may have been my first time altogether, given how satisfying I found that flick of his tongue on my nipple. Not that I minded that at any point, but it rarely did for me what it was doing now.

Tugging my top further down, his lips trailed to my other breast. It wasn't a gasp this time, but a moan. A deep, rumbling sound that echoed off the red, moonlit forest.

"Ds's da?" someone called. *Who's there?*

I couldn't begin to describe how, but somehow, those words automatically registered in my mind. I'd yet to attempt speaking this language aloud, but I knew it. Somehow, someway, I knew this language, and I understood every word that was spoken in each of these memories, each of these visions, even if the language was long dead by now.

"Who's there?" They spoke louder that time, firmer.

Pulling back, he gave a teasing half smile. One that I could hardly detect in the dim light. "Drogo, Mum."

"Fucking stars," she called back. "You nearly scared me half to death, boy. Have you seen Anise?"

I pressed my lips together to keep the laugh that tried to fall out trapped inside. He did the same before clearing his throat. "I think I saw her out with Rion. I'm sure she'll be home soon."

Those were our names then. Drogo and Anise.

I liked the ring that had to it.

"Well, if she's not back by the third moon's rising, you're going out there to find her!"

"Yes, ma'am," he called. Lowering his voice, he came in for another kiss, this one softer than the last. "How about a walk?"

"I'm quite happy"—holding his face in my hands, I leaned in and kissed him softly, slowly, but deeply—"right here."

"Even where my mum can hear us?" He chuckled, then kissed me again. "Come on."

Carefully, he set me on the ground. My feet sloshed into snow so high it reached my knees, but he took my hand and ran. He ran, and I ran with him, and I laughed, and I smiled, and he did too, and I had never felt so free in my life.

"This is where you're taking me?" Propping my hands on my hips, smiling, I eyed the igloo a few dozen strides ahead. That's all there was. An igloo amid a snowy plane, and a mountain far in the distance. The red moon was our only light, and there was something sensual about it. A bit odd, but sensual all the same. "This'll be a better place to kiss?"

"It's warm inside. That's gotta be better than kissing against a tree." Grinning like a child, or perhaps, like the child he was, Drogo walked backwards toward it.

I say *child* loosely. Maybe, by technicality, he was. I didn't know for certain. I'd yet to see or hear anyone mention his age in these visions, memories. But he couldn't have been more than twenty, and I imagined I was around that same age.

"I didn't mind the tree."

"You'll like this better."

Breathing out a dramatic sigh, I followed him. "If I don't?"

"You will."

Not to my surprise, nor the girl's mind I was in, I did like it better.

After ducking through the small, tunnel like entrance, vibrant blue and green and purple light shined. Heat all but boiled toward me. Boiling really was the word for it, because once inside, that's exactly what we were in.

A steaming, blue, green, and purple, almost party lit, hot tub. That's what it looked like, at least. Like something that, in the modern world, would be present at a celebrity house party.

What gave it that color? I couldn't be sure—Anise surely wasn't studying it—but it looked like some type of luminescent algae that lined the spring. Its glow wasn't blinding, but bright enough to light a dark room, a bit like the flash of a thousand fireflies in an empty field on a spring day.

"You've been here before," Drogo said.

"What?" I asked.

"You're not surprised." He gestured to the hot spring. "People are usually surprised when they see something like this."

I gave a half smile. "People, eh? Or pretty girls?"

"Pretty girls, are, in fact, people, you know."

Stepping past him, dodging an icicle as big as my head along the way, I basked in the heat that radiated from the steaming spring. As I sat, staring down at those vibrant lights, another image flashed.

Suddenly, I was in a hot spring like this, gazing down at the algae that glowed below, but my legs were smaller. Innocent, joyous laughter billowed from my lips and from those around me. A glance to my left revealed a little boy. He couldn't have been more than ten. His hair was black, dangling to the middle of his back, pulled back in a braid. Against his pearly white skin, his blue eyes glistened bright in the illuminance of the algae. Although his eyes were striking against his dark complexion, what stuck out about him, were his pointed ears. An Elf, I had to assume.

To his left, a little blonde girl sat. Blonde truly wasn't the right descriptor. It was as white as the snow of the igloo above our heads. Her eyes, an icy shade of blue. She smiled at me, laughing, splashing hot water my way.

To my right sat another little girl. Her skin was darker than ours, a warm, golden brown. Her bouncy black curls were wound into a tight knot at the back of her head. She laughed and shoved my shoulder, and I shoved hers.

Then the memory was gone, and a hollowness stretched through my stomach.

It wasn't a nostalgic type of hollowness, but a deep yearning. I missed them as deeply as I missed the mother who'd walked out on me in my current life. They weren't just friends, but people I cared for with my whole being. Almost family.

And they were gone.

I wasn't sure I wanted to see the part of the story that explained why or how that came to be.

Tugging off my boots, I shook my head at Drogo. "We found a spring like this when I was a girl. My friends and I, I mean. It was my favorite place in the world."

He took my hand and helped me onto my ass, smiling when I hiked up my skirt to dip my legs inside. "And?"

"And what?"

"I think you owe me then."

I got comfortable with my legs in the water and scoffed up at him. "And what am I supposed to owe you?"

Sitting beside me, he rolled up his pants and dipped his legs in as well. "An apology."

Another scoff, this one paired with a smile. "Why would I be apologizing?"

"Not wanting to see my igloo. And then liking it anyway."

Grabbing a fistful of his shirt, I yanked him into me and kissed him again. It was just as deep as that last one had been. So deep that he was panting by the time I pulled back.

I smirked. "That's the closest you're getting to an apology."

Releasing a breathy laugh, face flushed, he brushed some hair behind my ear. "Suppose I'll take it."

"I suppose you don't have much choice, do you?" Smiling, I pushed some hair behind his ear as well. Not pointed, just to clarify.

Smiling at me, the same boyish smile he gave me almost every day in the modern world, in my modern body, he leaned in. And he kissed me.

It was different than how he kissed me now. Not so hungry. Not so strong. Surely, he possessed the same strength as my Declan, if the memories where he transformed into a wolf and we ran together through the snow were any indication. But he was so tender with me in these memories. So much gentler.

I loved both. The tenderness of this moment as well as the ferocity of the ones Declan typically gave me.

As the kiss deepened, as his hand slid down my body, around my waist, drawing me closer to him, I found myself envying this girl. This old version of myself. The child I had been when we fell in love for the first time.

I wanted to be touched like this. So softly, so carefully. I wanted Declan to be this gentle with me. Why had he never been like this with me in the modern world? Of course, I never remembered asking him for gentleness. But I wasn't asking for it now either, and he simply did it.

Gradually, that hand on my waist drifted between my thighs. He only coasted the tips of his fingers between them at first, slowly trailing them closer to my cunt.

And when he did, I tensed. Not with an awkward discomfort, but with...

"What's the matter?" Lips still on mine, Drogo inched back. Our faces were so close that I could still feel his breath on my cheeks, his forehead against mine, but he lowered his hand. "Are you alright?"

Forcing a smile, I nodded. "I'm fine."

The tremble of my voice betrayed me.

Ever so slightly, Drogo pulled back some more. He removed his hand from my thighs entirely. He still sat close, but made sure there was at least a hair of distance between us now. "No, you're afraid."

"That's not it—"

"I can smell it, Anise." Frowning, he shook his head. "You don't have to do anything you don't want to."

"I do want to."

"You don't have to lie—"

"I *do* want to," I repeated, snatching his hand from his side and sliding it up my skirt. The cool feel of his fingers was shocking, and not in a pleasant way. And still, I said, "I swear, I do."

Instead of touching my pussy, he brought his hand to my inner thigh and worked his fingers up and down slowly. He made sure not to touch that sensitive spot. "Then what are you afraid of?"

"Drogo, I'm not—"

"Don't lie to me." The words may have sounded firm, but they were so gentle rolling off his tongue, so concerned. "If you're not ready for this, I'll wait. Whatever we're doing, I'm happy. We don't need to rush."

"I *am* ready," I insisted. "It's just... I want this. I want to give you this part of me." Damn, I was cheesy. "And I know you'll be careful. I know you won't try to, but it hurts, and I'm nervous."

Slowly, his head tilted. "Sex hurts?"

"Well, yes."

Anise—or I, rather—said that with such confidence, it hurt my heart.

Drogo looked just as puzzled, just as sad for her, as I was. "I know the first time does, but it shouldn't... You're not a virgin, are you?"

I made a noise that expressed my annoyance. "Of course not."

"And it hurts?" Still, he looked so confused. "Every time, it hurt you? He *always* hurt you?"

"It hurts us all," I said. I truly believed it, too. "It's different for men. It doesn't hurt you. You're *going* inside—you don't have someone jamming inside of you. Of course it hurts. But it's okay. I want that. I want you to feel good. So don't worry if I seem nervous. I want it."

"Oh, ol boaluahe." *My love.* What a horrible pet name. This language, it was so harsh. The opposite of romantic. *Love* sounded so much better than *ol boaluahe.* "It shouldn't. It's not supposed to hurt. Does it hurt when you do it yourself?"

"When I do it myself?"

Oh, you sweet child.

"When you..." Drogo let out a half laugh. At first, at least. A few seconds ticked by, and that sadness came back to his eyes, and all the humor left. "You've never enjoyed sex. Alone, or with someone else, you've *never* enjoyed it."

"Women don't. That's what my mum said." There was so much confidence in my voice when I spoke those words. How dare a man think they understood a woman's body better than I did? "Stop looking at me like I'm stupid."

Jesus Christ, she thought sex was *supposed* to hurt? She'd never climaxed? That's why she was scared?

This poor girl.

Frowning, he shook his head. "I don't think you're stupid, Anise. I just don't think you've ever been with somebody who cared about your pleasure."

I laughed at him. It was a quiet, annoyed little snort of a laugh, still so confident that he was wrong.

He laughed as well. "You don't believe me."

"I think women may have told you that they enjoyed it, but that doesn't mean that they did."

"Well, how about I do my best to show you how good it feels, and the moment it hurts you, or the moment you don't like it, you tell me to stop."

Smirking, I arched a brow. "We're betting then, eh?"

"I suppose so." His smile was far more devious than boyish this time. "Deal?"

"Deal."

Devious still, smirking, he leaned in for one more kiss. Then he pulled away, tugged his shirt over his head, and hopped into the water with a splash.

Laughing, I playfully smacked his shoulder. "You're getting me all wet."

"Oh, believe me, ol boaluahe." Grinning up at me, shaking the water off his damp brown curls, his fingertips found my thighs. Ever so slightly, he inched my dress up my lap until cold snow touched the backs of my thighs. As he nudged them apart, then kissed my knee, butterflies flapped in my belly. Big brown eyes smiling up at me, he stretched my legs a bit wider. "You'll be dripping soon."

Another chuckle escaped me. "What're you doing?"

"You'll see." He stretched my legs even wider, pressing another kiss to my inner thigh. "Just relax."

"I *am* relaxed."

He dipped lower in the water, draping my knees over his shoulders. Again, he tugged my knees apart. "You're quite tense, actually."

"I am not—"

His fingers slipped all the way to my cunt, and he gently traced a fingertip down my slit.

A soft sigh fell from my lips, pleasure building from that one touch.

"*Now* you're relaxing," he murmured, kissing my thigh again. The stiffness of my legs eased over his shoulders when he did it again, traveling further and further north. His finger kept tracing slowly from my clit to my cunt, but that was all he gave me. The most ginger caress. Enough to make me gasp, enough to make me feel good, but not close to enough to make me climax. "This doesn't hurt, does it?"

Everything else he'd said had a smart ass edge to it. Not that. It was genuine concern.

Gulping in a breath, holding it there, I shook my head.

"Does it feel good?" he whispered, kissing again, this time only inches from my pussy.

I nodded.

With a smile, he kissed one more time. "Now lean back, and just breathe, ol boaluahe."

I swallowed. "What're you doing?"

"Aside from making you feel good?" he asked. I nodded, but he didn't respond. That hand that'd been teasing my cunt came to my hips. He hauled me closer to him, ducking lower. Eyes still one mine, he kissed again, but this time, on my clit. When I heaved in a breath, he let his tongue sneak through. Gently, slowly, he traced the tip in a circle around my clit. My mouth dropped with pleasure, awed by just how magnificent that felt. He kissed again, this time with no tongue, then whispered against me, "Tasting you."

My eyes eased open. A white popcorn ceiling stared back at me, lit by the early morning, boring, yellow sun. The ceiling fan overhead spun, casting a chill over me.

Damn it.

Of all the times to wake up, it had to be then? Sure, my hand was in my pants, but that was nothing compared to Drogo's tongue.

But it wasn't even the pleasure of that dream that made it so intense. We'd barely gotten to the fun part.

It was the intimacy. No matter how much I liked my self care, I couldn't feel *that* on my own. The connection between Drogo and Anise, the chemistry and tenderness, was what I craved.

And lucky for me, the modern Drogo hugged me from behind. Also lucky for me, his length was already firm against my ass.

Rolling over, I touched my lips to his. He grumbled something indistinguishable, and I kissed him again. At his lips, I whispered, "Baby."

Another grumble.

Kissing again, I lifted a leg around his hips and ground against him. His hand found my waist. He kissed me back, but nuzzled closer. Hopefully because he didn't realize what I was trying to do and not because he was turning me down.

"Baby," I whispered against his lips.

"Hm?" Bringing my waist closer to his, he kissed me again, but stayed in his early morning haze.

No use in beating around the bush. "Can you fuck me?"

That woke him up. Eyes opening, he stifled a yawn. "What?"

I laughed. "I had a dream about you."

Arching a brow, yawning again, he gave a sleepy smirk. "About fucking me?"

"Mhmm." I kissed him again, just as the soft as the last had been. "And now I *really* wanna live it."

"Hmm." Growing more awake by the heartbeat, he dipped that hand from my waist to the waistband of my sweats. When he touched my pussy, his smile stretched wider. "Damn, that dream must've been hot as hell. You're dripping."

Tingles stretched from my belly deep into my cunt. "It wasn't that hot."

He arched that brow again, tracing his fingertips slowly over my clit and nudging my pants down my legs. "I think you're lying."

The euphoria of that touch clenched all those muscles deep inside. Kicking my pants the rest of the way off, I managed out, "No, it was, but it was…"

His speed picked up, making me gasp and arch closer to him. "But it was…?"

"Romantic," I moaned, reaching between us to stroke him. He was rock hard now, which only made me want him more.

"Romantic, huh?" Sliding one finger into me, his thumb found my clit. "Tell me more."

I laughed, working him up and down slowly. "It… It wasn't a *dream*. It was a memory, I think."

"Yeah?" Declan's smile widened. Faster than I could register what was happening, I was on my back, and he was overtop of me. In the blink of an eye, he plunged in so deep, so hard, that I gasped. "What'd I do to you, sweetheart?"

Kissing him again, holding his cheek softly when I did, I swallowed. Suddenly I was that young girl again, alone with him in the igloo, nervous. Nervous for what exactly, I didn't know. Not getting to feel how she did, maybe?

Stopping deep inside me, Declan tugged back just far enough to look at me. "What's the matter?"

Deja vu.

"Nothing. Nothing's the matter. It's just…" Searching for the words, swallowing again, I trailed my fingers down his jaw. My voice came out far softer than I was used to. "It was our first time, I think. You were so gentle with me."

Eyes softening, he smiled. "Do you want me to be gentle with you now?"

My cheeks burned hot.

Why? Why was I embarrassed? It was exactly what I wanted. I wanted him to be as sweet and soft to me as Drogo had been with Anise, so why wouldn't those words leave my lips?

All I could do was nod.

And the smile he gave me when I admitted that, the light that shined in his eyes, was just as beautiful as it'd been when he smiled up at me from that glowing water. Like he wanted to hear me say that as much as I wanted to feel the intimacy we'd had all those years ago.

So gingerly, he leaned down and kissed me. Rocking his hips into me, lips travelling to my neck, he whispered in my ear, "Tell me about our first time, sweetheart."

Coiling my legs around his hips, I basked in the comfort of his warm skin against mine. "I... I thought it'd hurt."

"Because I was so big?"

I laughed, and he joined in, but he kept the rhythm of his soft, gentle thrusts. "Maybe. I woke up before I got to that part."

Still kissing my neck, he dipped all the way in. Rather than a thrust, he ground against me, letting his pelvis rock against my clit, massaging something magnificent inside me with the head of his cock, bringing me just as much pleasure as Drogo had in that dream. "Why then?"

"I..." A moan cut me off. I curled my arms around his back, taking in every inch of his skin beneath my fingertips. "I wasn't a virgin, but that's what I thought sex was like. I thought it was supposed to hurt. You..." The pleasure of his weight grinding on my clit pulled me from my thoughts once more.

Tugging back enough to look at me, he propped himself up on one hand. He tucked some hair away from my face, eyes gentle. "That's really sad."

That tenderness, that compassion, only added to the bliss of his touch. "But you bet me that you'd make me feel good."

His smile returned. "Did I?"

"Mhmm," I murmured. I described the setting in a bit more detail, explaining the hot spring we were in. While he didn't thrust faster at that, I swore I felt him get even harder inside of me. "Then you got inside, and you kissed up my thighs, and... Fuck, you feel so good."

And he really did. He was as deep inside me as he could get, grinding, then rotating his hips. Not just fucking me, but practically massaging every inch of my pussy with his cock.

"And what, sweetheart?" he murmured, breaths hard, panting.

Finding his cheek, I trailed a finger to his lips and traced the tip of mine along the bottom one. A soft moan parted his lips, eyes so focused, so aroused, which only turned me on more. "You tasted me."

"God damn, Brooke," he groaned, attempting to pull back. But the soft groan that fell from his lips told me he attempted a moment too late. His cock throbbed, making my cunt do the same. The heat of his cum filled my cunt. "Fuck, I'm sorry."

"Don't apologize," I moaned.

Not only was I on the pill, but I fucking *loved* that feeling. The contractions, the warmth, but most of all, the look on his face. Knowing that I turned him on, that I brought him there, was the sexiest thing for me. It made me feel wanted, desired, and beautiful.

Especially like this. When the moment was deeper than rough, gritty fucking. This was heartfelt, emotional, and for a reason I couldn't put into words, feeling his cum overflow my cunt made me feel so complete.

"You know what I want?" he murmured, kissing me softly.

"What's that?" I whispered.

"To taste..." His lips trailed down my chest, kissing my nipple as he traveled all the way to my pussy. Then, just as Drogo had, he kissed my clit. When I gasped, he said, "My cum mixed with yours."

"Jesus Christ," was all I had time to say before he grabbed both of my thighs and dove in.

This man didn't *taste* my cunt. He fucking devoured it. His tongue moved so fast over my clit, from side to side, then in a circle, then up and down, until I was squirming beneath his hold.

But when I squirmed, when my body involuntarily quivered, he'd slow just enough for me to catch my breath. Then he'd go back to flicking his tongue around like a vibrator.

It was no different this time. All the moans he let out, all the pleasure he was giving me, just circled back to himself. We were an endless loop of pleasure. Like turning me on, bringing me to brink, holding me there on the edge, was just as erotic for him as it was for me.

I could only hope that Drogo gave Anise as much as Declan was giving me now, because everyone deserved to feel this. The immense pleasure tied up with comfort and familiarity.

That was intimacy, wasn't it? Opening your body for someone else, giving them the opportunity to treat you however they wished, only for them to give you the best you'd ever felt. To make you feel wanted, and safe, and—

"Fuck, I'm gonna come," I practically screamed.

Holding me by both of my thighs, he brought me as close to him as space allowed and did his best fucking work. I didn't even know *what* he was doing. Only that the heat of his mouth was against me, moving with impeccable speed and precision, and I loved every fucking second of it.

Stars flickered against my eyes when the contractions took hold. He didn't stop when they came, but maintained the perfect rhythm. As I came, through my mind flashed the image of the two of us in that spring, and no matter how wonderful that memory was, this one was just as beautiful. It would stick with me for lifetimes to come as well.

Because it was more than just sex. It was the most intense, affectionate sex we'd ever had.

When the contractions slowed, and I stopped screaming, Declan gave my clit one more kiss. I shivered, and he chuckled. Sitting forward, wiping his lip, he smiled. "Was that romantic enough for you, sweetheart?"

Laughing, I hauled him toward me. With another kiss, I nodded. "That was perfect."

"*You're* perfect." He kissed me again. "And the way you taste—"

A bang sounded.

I jumped.

He held me closer, pressing a finger over my lips.

Another bang, this one louder than the last. Not like the swinging of the door when Ria came in early, but like someone had just flipped my dining table.

That's not Ria, is it? I said in his mind.

Shaking his head, he eyed the doorway. *Sure as shit doesn't smell like Ria.*

CHAPTER EIGHT

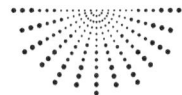

EMORY

"I'm not paying for it." Pouting beneath his white beard, Andrew crossed his arms against his chest. "It tastes like shit, man. Try it. I dare you."

"Jesus, I told you I'd make you a new one." Emory tossed his dirty dish rag to the counter, unphased when some water splashed Andrew's shirt. He was in no god damned mood today. "But if you send it back again, you can piss up a rope, dude. I'm not gonna do this all night."

"Where's Declan?" He glanced past Emory through the serving hatch behind the bar. "Since someone's got an attitude, let me talk to—"

"He's not here." Before Andrew could continue bitching, as he always did, Emory snapped, "And no, I'm not calling him. He's got enough on his plate right now, and he doesn't need to hear about how you're not satisfied with the third drink I've made you."

And, just as he said it, Declan's full plate of problems walked in the front door.

Wearing a baggie sweatshirt and tight blue jeans, black hair tossed into a messy bun, blue eyes twinkling around pin-pricked pupils, Ariana Lewis walked in that front door like nothing had happened. Like she was as innocent as ever.

Declan didn't know that Ria was to blame for the current clusterfuck he was dealing with, but Emory did. Emory knew because he knew Ria better than Declan did—better than her sister did, better than Declan did—probably better than anyone.

Andrew was still ranting as Emory started around the bar. Unable to stop his flaring nostrils, unable to return Ria's smile, he stalked across the room as if his feet were on fire, practically leaving a trail of flames in his wake. And still, she smiled at him.

"Hey, you," she said, lifting her purse higher on her shoulder. "Andrew giving you a hard time ag—"

"We need to talk." Emory snatched her by her upper arm and started toward the back of the house.

"Excuse the hell out of you." Not strong enough to physically remove his hand from her bicep, she teleported a foot or two back. Glaring, she tucked her arms against her chest. "You wanna talk, we can talk, but don't put your fucking hands on me like that. That hurt."

Releasing his tight fist was no easy feat. Emory clenched his jaw to compensate.

He hadn't meant to hurt her. He rarely meant to hurt anyone. But Angel strength was intense. So was their brash, cold nature. The irony was, Declan was the Werewolf. Some would think that he'd be the one with an all but uncontrollable temper. An animalistic rage. That wasn't the case at all.

No. Declan was a smartass, but rarely violent. His touch was careful at all times. But Emory? Emory couldn't count how many times he'd shattered a glass by simply holding it too tightly.

He could've done the same to Ria. Never would've forgiven himself if he had.

But damn it, he had the right to be pissed right now.

"I'm sorry. I didn't mean to. But we *need* to talk."

"Alright, let's talk."

CHAPTER NINE

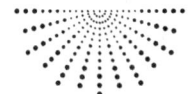

RIA

"Why the fuck did you lie?" Emory leaned against the door of the cramped office in the back of Spades. Ria had her back to a cluttered desk, bills and membership ledgers piled on top of it. Her back was practically against the wall. Which would've meant Emory was caging her in, if not for the fact that she could—and would—teleport out of here the moment she was done with his shit. "Dipping, I get. Avoiding the cops if you had something to do with this, I get. But lying to Brooke? To Declan? Why, Ari? What the fuck did you do?"

That hurt.

Deep in her chest, that hurt. All of this hurt.

Yes, she did know Alicia, and yes, she had lied about it. But not because she wanted to make this any worse. It hurt that Emory thought she'd intentionally harm anyone she cared about. It hurt that he couldn't see that she was doing her best here.

Even him calling her Ari, which usually made her chest warm, hurt. She wasn't sure why he did that. Called her Ari. Brooke had called her Ria her whole life, so had everyone else. No one called her Ari.

On one of their not so uncommon late night drinking sessions while he was closing up Spades, Emory asked what Ria was short for. Ariana, she'd told him. Giving that teasing smile of his, he'd said, "And of all the nicknames, you go by Ria? Why not Ari? You're pretty, you should have a pretty nickname."

And thus, Ari.

That was the first time she could remember getting butterflies. Maybe she'd had them before, but never like that. Never from someone she trusted. Never from a friend.

That's who Emory was.

No matter how beautiful his brown eyes were, no matter how much she loved that coppery hair, no matter how attractive she found him, he was her friend. A friend who preferred men to women, a friend who showed his affection in a tough love sort of way and was a little rough around the edges, despite the flamboyant stereotypes of queer men.

A friend who would always remain just that. A friend.

One who was pissed at her. If there was anyone whose good graces she wanted to stay in, it was his. And yet, he glared at her now like she was the scum of the earth.

It took everything she had to keep her voice level. "I didn't do anything—"

"Bullshit. You knew her, Ari. You knew that dead girl, and you lied about it to the people who care about you the most." Nostrils flared, jaw tight, he spoke through gritted teeth. "And I know you stole money out of the drawer last week, too. I covered for you, because if Declan found out, your ass would be in jail. But you couldn't have just asked me for it? You had to steal again? When you could've just fucking asked me, and I would've given it to you?"

She was trying so hard to keep herself together, but that ache in her chest stretched wider. All she could manage out was, "I'm sorry." It came out strained, hardly more than a whisper.

"For what?" Emory barked that question, and Ria flinched. He didn't notice. Or maybe he was too pissed to care. "Killing that girl? Or doing it behind your sister's boyfriend's bar?"

Shaking her head, Ria fought like hell to contain the tears that threatened her eyes. "I would never do that."

"Then what the fuck did you do, Ari? Jesus fucking Christ, how deep are you? What the fuck's going on?"

How deep was she?

She was at the bottom of the ocean. There was no light here. There was only darkness. Darkness, and regret, and grief, and no matter how hard she paddled, she couldn't get out. The weight of all that water, all that pain, was crushing her, and she didn't know how she was still vertical from all the pressure.

Desperately, she wanted to say so. She wanted to tell him. Tell *anyone.* Tell him exactly what happened, exactly how deep she was, but that depth caught up to her. But the words lodged in her throat, drowned by the weight of it all. All that water escaped through her eyes instead.

A quiet sob breaking through her lips, she cupped her hands before her face. Shaking her head, Ria tried to stay as quiet as possible. She failed that attempt.

Something between shock and sympathy fell over Emory's face. Eyes wide, forehead creased, frowning, he found her fingers. Tugging them from her face with one hand, he thumbed her tears with the other. When that didn't stop her cries, he whispered, "Come here," and wrapped his arms around her.

Then he held her. He held her so tightly that, even if only for a few heartbeats, she didn't feel like she was drowning anymore. He traced his hands over her back, murmuring a soft, "shh," sound, resting his head against hers.

Safe. Here, now, she was safe.

But she wasn't. Alicia wasn't, either. Alicia was dead.

Alicia was dead.

Just when she thought she could stop sobbing, that the ocean atop her had finally stopped leaking from her eyes, the thought of Alicia—poor, dead, Alicia—brought another glass shattering shriek from her lips. Thank gods the music was loud, or she'd have died of embarrassment.

Considering the way Alicia died, maybe that wouldn't be such a bad way to go. Embarrassment was better than violent vitriol. Anything was better than how Alicia died. Anything.

As had become habit in the last twenty-four hours, Ria moved herself from heartbroken to numb. No matter how much she wanted to enjoy this, to find comfort in Emory's touch, ease and tranquility escaped her. She felt the soothing touch of his hands on her back, heard his quiet hushing, and allowed the pain, and the peace, to leave.

It was better she felt nothing than to feel what she had felt a moment ago.

When she stopped crying, Emory pulled back to look at her. He still held her upper arms, staring deeply into her eyes. Not a romantic, loving stare. More like how a mother looked at her infant when they momentarily stopped breathing. As if to say, "Don't you ever fucking do that again because I'll kill you if you die on me."

"You have to tell me what's going on, Ari," he said. "I'm not letting you out of this room until you do."

Like he could keep her here.

Ria almost rolled her eyes at that, but she swallowed hard instead. While those tears had been real, from here out, it was an act. If Ria had learned anything throughout her life, it was that men were easy to manipulate. So long as she looked innocent enough, sweet enough, she could get exactly what she needed from them. Fawning. That was Ria's best defense mechanism.

"I didn't hurt Alicia," Ria said, voice sheepish. "She was my friend. I loved her." She didn't need to make her words tremble. They did so all on their own. "But I did take the money from the drawer. And I know it was wrong, and I'm really sorry, but I—"

"I don't give a shit about the money." Emory grabbed her cheek and thumbed a tear away. That sounded like a sweet sentence, perhaps even romantic, but his touch was as brash as his voice. Maybe his intention had been to hold Ria's cheek gingerly, to comfort her, but Ria suspected she'd have a bruise where his thumb was by the day's end. "I give a shit about you. The fact that your friend—a girl you work with in a dangerous fucking job—was beaten to death and dumped *here*. Did you witness it? If you didn't do it, you must've seen it happen, or you wouldn't be the mess that you are right now. Was it a john?"

Yes. Ria had witnessed it. She'd tried to stop him, and that was why she was in one of Brooke's sweaters now. One that'd cover all the evidence of her struggle. "No. It wasn't a john. But I've got it under control. Don't worry about—"

"I'm gonna worry about you whether you like it or not. And you didn't answer my first qu—"

"Because it doesn't matter!" Ria shoved Emory's hand from her face. She wasn't strong enough to do so purely with her hand, so a bit of telekinesis helped.

It helped push his hand away, at least. It made *this* worse. Because Emory wasn't giving her that freaked out, overprotective, angry face anymore. His forehead creased, mouth opening ever so slightly.

Hurt. He was hurt that she had pushed him away. Hurt that he had covered her ass, and surely expected him to continue doing so, only to push him away. Emory risked everything to protect Ria. His job. His best friend, practically his brother. And Ria all but spit in his face.

That wasn't fair. She hated herself for it. Hated the damage she was doing to the relationship with her best friend, her sister, and even her sister's relationship.

But what other choice did she have?

She didn't. Put plainly, Ria had no other choice. Lying, pushing everyone she cared for away, was how it had to be this time. Not for her sake, but for theirs.

Ria would fix this. But she couldn't if they were all watching her. If they knew what was happening, it'd only get worse. So much worse.

She couldn't let them wind up like Alicia. She *couldn't.*

"I'll replace the money," Ria said after a quiet moment. "I promise I will. You know I pay my debts."

"Jesus fucking Christ, how many times do I have to tell you this? I don't care about the money. I care about *you.* I care that you're fucking terrified."

"I'm fine. So stop. Just stop, alright?" Grabbing her purse off the end table, she started toward the door. "Everything's fine—"

Again, Emory wrapped a hand around her bicep. This time, he did what Ria had expected him to do since this conversation had started. "Tell me the truth, Ari."

His Angel powers took hold. Involuntarily, Ria's mouth dropped open. The story, the background, the memories from last night, from a few months prior when it all began, was like vomit in her throat. Emory's touch urged it to fall from her lips, but the spell she had cast on herself this morning did its job.

The words were there. Right there in her throat. But she managed to swallow them down.

She teleported out of his grasp.

Landing in her van parked outside Spades, those words dropped from her lips in a sob. It rippled out of her so quickly, Emory wouldn't have been able to understand it all anyway.

But the spell did its job. It gave her enough time to get away.

Now, the worst part was, until this was over, until she cleaned up her mess, she couldn't see Emory again. Because next time, he'd have some morion on hand. The gem would keep her from teleporting, Emory wouldn't give her the chance to run, and she'd tell him everything.

But until it was over, she couldn't tell him a damn word.

CHAPTER TEN

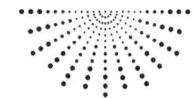

EMORY

Dropping his head to his hands, rubbing his eyes, Emory released a slow, calming breath.

This was bad. Whatever it was, it was fucking *bad*. He didn't know what to do. Which friend should he hold allegiance for? Ria? Declan? Brooke?

They were all on the same team. They had to be. Even when they bickered and fought, they were always on the same team. Was that still true?

Surely Ria hadn't dumped the body here. What purpose would that serve? She loved Brooke more than anything, cared for Declan just as much, and certainly didn't want Emory penalized for the missing cash.

No, someone had a gun to her head. She didn't dump that body behind the bar. She didn't cause this, but she knew who did. Emory would get it out of her. Then he'd make the bastard who put Ria in this position wish he'd never fucking met her.

A knock rapped on the door. Emory's heart skipped. A silly fantasy, but maybe it was her. Maybe she'd come back.

Ria's pretty face wasn't the one that greeted him when he opened the office door. Instead, it was a crotchety old man in a suit. At first, Emory didn't recognize him. He had green eyes, a graying mustache, a balding head, and a plump figure. But he recognized the badge he flashed right away. *Detective Tyler.*

"Customers gotta stay at the front of the house." Emory glanced that way. "But sorry, no coffee and donuts. And no boys in blue discount."

"I'm here on business." Detective Tyler glowered at Emory. "Have you seen Declan today?"

"Yup."

Tyler looked past him into the office. Emory didn't attempt to block his view. There was nothing to hide at Spades. Aside from the fact that Tyler was the only human in here. "He here?"

"Nope."

"Any idea where he is?"

Emory glanced at his watch. "Well, it's five thirty, so if I had to guess, fucking his girl. Five's their happy hour."

Tyler didn't seem to appreciate Emory's sarcasm. Emory didn't appreciate cops.

"Too bad. Was hoping to get a word in." Tugging his notebook from his pocket, he clicked a pen. "You were here last night, weren't you?"

"Yup."

"You see Declan last night?"

"Yup."

"You see him go outside?"

"Nope."

"Not once."

"Nope."

Huffing, Tyler straightened up. "Would you rather do this at the station?"

"You gonna arrest me?" Emory leaned against the doorframe. "Or just hold me for questioning until I lawyer up? You know good and damn well that we had nothing to do with that girl's death."

Forcing himself into releasing his tight jaw, Tyler traced his tongue along his teeth. "Look, I'm trying to find Alicia's family some closure—"

"Bullshit." Emory laughed. "Bullshit, dude. How many girls like her get killed a month around here? How many of those girls' families get closure? You don't give a fuck about her. You just care about taking Declan down. Sorry to break it to you, but he's not a murderer. He's not a dope dealer like his dad. He's a good guy all the way around. So look somewhere else, because he's not your fucking guy."

Emory started past Tyler, but the detective caught him by the shoulder.

His grip tight on Emory, he spoke low. "Maybe he didn't kill Alicia. But Alicia's not the only body that's turned up in connection to this place. She's just the only one left somewhere we could find."

With furrowed brows, Emory spun around to face him. "What the hell are you talking about?"

"Ryan Taylor. Olivia Martinez. Eric Evans. Ethan Walker. All reported missing since Declan's taken over this place. None found," Tyler said. "Don't even get me started on the list associated with his daddy. But that son of a bitch's dead now. Can't do shit about it. Here's the thing, though. Declan looks better on paper. But ya know what I think?"

Emory's stomach was in knots.

Eric, yes, Declan had killed. The prick deserved it, but that was moot. Declan had killed that man, and Tyler was determined to prove it. Still, Emory had no trouble sounding natural when he said, "What's that?"

"Declan's just smarter than his daddy." Tyler smirked. "He thought if he stayed out of drugs, trafficking, guns, and all that, he'd keep the heat off himself. But see, I remember that fucker. I remember how good he was at getting rid of evidence. It might be harder for me to prove, but have no doubt, boy." They were almost chest to chest now, Tyler's eyes flicking quickly between Emory's, scrutinizing his every breath. "I know a killer when I see one. And I'm gonna put all the fuel I've got on this fire. It's not gonna fizzle out this time."

He gave Emory's shoulder a hard squeeze, smiled once more, and said, "You have a good night, Emory."

CHAPTER ELEVEN

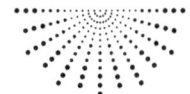

DECLAN

I held a finger over my lips, motioning for Brooke to stay silent. With a glare, she ducked beside me next to the doorframe. She tied her robe around her waist, a pretty red silk one. Under different circumstances, I would have complimented her on it.

Another bang sounded from in the house.

Living room, I believed. Living room or entryway. But as the thump of footsteps pounded closer, approaching the bedroom, I snuck a peek through the crack between the door and its frame. A man. A man roughly my size, which wasn't all that common.

He wore jeans and a black hoodie. He sauntered into Ria's room on the opposite side of the hall, his back to me. I couldn't have made out his face. But it was the opportunity I needed.

Grabbing Brooke by her waist, I rushed her to the wall behind the door. She swatted at me. *Put your hands on me again, Declan.*

I rolled my eyes and went back to the other side of the room. *You say that like I assaulted you.*

You manhandled me, which isn't all that different.

There's a fucking intruder in your house. Who was now exiting Ria's room and coming toward us. Short blond hair, strong jaw, thick beard.

Somewhere between my age and thirty. *And he's coming this way. Follow my lead.*

Yes, sir.

The sarcasm was palpable, even in thought form.

Footsteps heavy, now close enough that I could see his pinpricked pupils, I pulled in a deep breath and held it there. I didn't let it go until he'd walked through the doorway.

Lunging behind him, I hooked an arm around his throat. He gasped, jammed me in the gut with his elbow, even tried stomping on my foot like women were taught to do with their high heels in self-defense classes. All of which accomplished nothing. We were the same size, but he wasn't a Werewolf. His strength was no different than a human's.

The smell of him suggested otherwise, however. Like a nursing home. That's how he smelled. Not to say he smelled like shit, or like death, or like cleaning agents.

Old. He smelled older than dirt.

"Vamp, huh?" I asked at his ear, holding his throat closer when he squirmed. "Funny, I thought you guys were pretty strong too."

He grunted, or maybe groaned, but I didn't release my hold.

"Here's how this is gonna go," I said, still close to his ear, looking at Brooke out of the corner of my eye. "My girl, she's gonna get some silver chains. We're gonna tie you to that chair in the corner. And you're gonna answer all our questions. You understand?"

It was stupid of me to expect some decency when I released my hold on his neck to let him answer. "Fuck you."

Before I could say a word, Brooke appeared in front of us. She snatched his hands from his sides and wrapped a rope of metal around his wrists. He squealed, and I held his throat tight enough to cut off his ability to do just that.

"He's weak because he's doped out of his god damned mind," Brooke said, winding the metal tighter and tighter around his wrists. "But there's no way in hell this is a coincidence." She snatched the arm chair from the corner of the room and set it in front of me. "Sit his ass down and keep him there. Let me find some more chains."

Two hours.

She'd been torturing this man for two hours, and *I* was ready to beg for mercy. Also kind of aroused.

That wasn't to say that I enjoyed watching people being tortured. A bit of a sadist, I may have been. Tying Brooke up and pulverizing her pussy while I slapped her ass until it was blood red, I liked. But that was a sexual, romantic release. It had more to do with the power and control in that one area of my life than it did with violence itself.

But seeing Brooke like this?

Her hands were drenched in blood. The poor guy had a hole carved into the center of his chest. He received that when Brooke asked him what his name was, and he refused to answer. Instead of stabbing him, she chiseled slowly in a circle just above his heart. When he screamed, when he begged her to stop, for her to not kill him, she simply said, "Tell me your name."

Oliver. That was his name.

She filleted a piece of flesh of his arm. Like gutting a fish. It still hung there, flipped back like an extra sleeve that she'd rolled up. When it started to regrow, as Vampires did, she just sliced it again.

It was weird. I studied her closely as she did it. I could see it from the look on her face, she wasn't enjoying it. She got no release from it.

But she didn't stop either. She was ruthless, terrifying, and somehow fucking gorgeous at the same time.

I didn't know how she did it. Tortured. Never once had I tortured someone. Killed, yes, because I had to, but it was never about fun for me.

And that's what was so bizarre here. She wasn't enjoying it, but holy shit, she was good at it.

"Why were you in my sister's room?" Brooke asked. She had a fistful of his hair in her hand, craning his head as far back as possible to meet her gaze. "What the hell are you doing here? Is it about her? Is this about Ria?"

Sobbing, the man shook his head. "I don't know Ria."

Brooke lifted the blade to his neck and sliced quickly across it. Her knowledge of anatomy must've been excellent, because she only went deep enough to maim. Not murder.

"Keep lying to me," she said. "I can do this all day. I think the longest I've tortured someone was about thirty-six hours. By then,"—she laughed, but it was hollow—"I was so delirious. I was trying to slice his leg, and I cut off a ball."

There went all of my arousal.

"Ended up killing the guy. Really wish I hadn't, because he did have information that I needed. But apparently, he wasn't giving it up. So, I did what I had to do." Grabbing a hold of his cheeks, pinching them between her thumb and forefinger, she stared deeply into his eyes. "If you think I won't do it again, you're an idiot. Half an inch deeper, and you'd be dead. So answer my god damned question. Why were you in Ria's room?"

The skin on his neck had mended, at least partly, and he was able to sob again. "I swear, I don't know her."

"Alright then. If you're not gonna talk, you're useless." Brooke lifted the blade high into the air, ready to plunge into his chest.

But just as she lowered it, he screamed, "Stop!"

"I think you need to give her a reason," I said, crossing my legs and straightening on the bed. "Looks like she's running out of patience."

"When it comes to my family?" Holding the tip of the blade to the center of his chest, she gave the most gruesome smile. "I'd kill for them. I'd die for them. If you don't give me a good god damned reason for why you're here, I'll prove it."

And suddenly, it all made sense.

That's why she was able to do this. No, this wasn't sexual to Brooke. No, it wasn't satisfying. No, she got no joy out of it.

It was survival. That's what this was to her. Torturing this man, torturing all of the people she had for the Chambers, it was about doing what she had to do in order to survive. Protect her sister. Protect herself. Pay the bills however possible.

Her determination to survive. Her fear of losing the person she cared about most. Her baby sister.

That was what she sold when she worked for the Chambers. Her soul, maybe. That's what she had to give up to survive.

"I needed money, alright?" Oliver said. "Davey. That's his name. I met him at my dealer's house. He asked me if I wanted to make some cash. Said he'd get me some dope. All I had to do was come here and wreck your place. Make you scared. But I swear, I don't know you. I don't know your sister. I just want to get high, man. I was so sick, and I just needed to get high. I'm sorry. I'm so, so sorry."

There it was.

Through all this, Brooke had shown no emotion. But now, there was the faintest glimmer of sympathy in her eyes. Probably for the same reason there had been that vicious hate a moment prior. Because he was an addict. Because she saw her baby sister in him. Because of the countless times Ria would've done anything to get high.

And then, as quickly as her sympathy had come, it was gone. That hard, emotionless face was back again.

Pushing the tip of the blade into Oliver's chest, barely enough to draw blood, she said, "Where's Davey live?"

Crying, Oliver shook his head. "I don't know."

Brooke pushed the tip of the blade in further. She stayed steady, unwavering as he cried for her to stop. She didn't though. She hadn't stopped once when he begged her to. "You don't know? Or you don't want to tell me?"

"I can't!" Writhing, trembling in his chains, Oliver shook his head once more. He shook his head so hard that I was almost certain his neck would break, and it would go flying across the room like a bowling ball. "You know I can't! He'll kill me. If I tell you anything, he'll fucking kill me!"

Again, Brooke only pushed the tip of the blade in deeper. It was a little more than an inch in there now. I had no idea how she was pulling it off. His ribs were right there. But for all I know, that sadistic beauty was pushing the blade in right between them, intentionally avoiding the bone. "You don't think I will?"

Another heart-wrenching sob. "Please. Please, just let me go. I told you everything I—"

Yanking the blade from his chest, she slammed it into his shoulder instead. She waited until he stopped screaming to continue. "No, you didn't. You didn't tell me where Davey lived. You didn't tell me where your dealer lives. Give me one of those answers and I'll let you go. We can pretend this never happened, Oliver. But if you don't give me something soon, I'm going to put this blade through your fucking heart and let my boyfriend eat it off the tip."

I grimaced. I had never eaten a person, although I'd been told by other Werewolves that it was a pleasant experience. Vampires, though? I wasn't so sure about. I imagined they tasted as old as they smelled.

Either way, I would only do that if I had to. Drinking their blood was one thing. Consuming the flesh was a whole other.

"You know what happens to people who snitch?" Oliver finally looked up on his own, brown eyes red with tears. "It'd be better if you did it than if they did."

"I'm not a cop," Brooke snapped. "That's who you don't snitch to, dip shit. I just want to know why this guy sent you to my god damned house.

And since you're not gonna answer that question, I don't have another option but to go out and find him myself."

Wrapping her fingers around the blade, she yanked it from his shoulder. He screamed again, but she paid him no mind. She rushed the blade back toward his chest.

But he screamed out, "Wait!" Just before the silver made impact. "Off the highway up north. I don't know the address, but I can show you the route. A-and my memories of the place, if you need them. It's quiet. Secluded. That's where my dealer lives. Davey's there a lot. We met a few times, but I don't know where he lives. He could live there, with him, for all I know. But if you stay there long enough, you'll find them. I swear you will."

While I was unfamiliar with that area, evidently Brooke wasn't. Because with a sigh, she straightened. Dropping the blade to the ground, she nodded my way. "You know if you're lying to me, he can track you down."

Swallowing, Oliver nodded.

"Alright then." She leaned down and loosened the chains around his wrists and ankles. As she stood back up, she turned my way. "Should probably get a shower before he walks outta here, huh?"

"Not a bad idea." I stood as well. "Want me to babysit?"

"You're the best." On her way past, she gave me a kiss on the cheek, then walked to the bathroom off the edge of the bedroom.

Once she was out of sight, I went to Oliver and helped him finish unwinding the chains.

"And here I was thinking you'd be the one to torture me," he said.

"Yeah, well. We all have our strong suits, and those are hers."

CHAPTER TWELVE

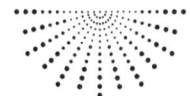

Oliver

Cunt, Oliver thought. He still felt Declan's eyes on his back as he tapped his cigarettes on his wrist. Didn't turn back though, even when he lifted one from the pack and brought it to his lips.

Fishing around in his pocket for the lighter, he was just grateful to have made it out of there alive. Quite a few times while that was occurring, he was almost certain that he wouldn't.

How could she justify something like that? Sure, Oliver was an intruder, but he hadn't caused any real harm. All he had done was break a few pictures, flip some furniture, and knocked over her bookshelf.

Which didn't matter all that much anyway. Because after she finished torturing him and got a shower, she made him clean it all up. Got him a dustpan and a garbage bag and everything. When he missed a spot, she made sure to tell him so.

Then, much to his surprise, she made him bathe. While she burned his clothes in the fireplace, Declan watched him from the toilet. He wasn't exactly eager to do that job, Oliver could tell, but the fact remained. Afterward, she made him clean his own blood off her hardwoods.

While that sort of treatment was absurd, it topped his list of tortures. Because yes, Oliver had a list.

More than once, somebody tied him to a chair and poked and prodded until he gave them the information they were looking for. That was why he traveled so much. There were a thousand vampire nests and werewolf packs, even a few guardians and Fae, all around the world who had a vendetta against him.

But that... That was the strangest one. Usually, Oliver got the boot as soon as he gave up the information they wanted. Not a shower and an unpaid cleaning service.

Halfway down the block now, the bright sun shined in Oliver's eyes. Warm, spring wind drifted over his skin, and yet, he was still cold. So cold.

So cold, in fact, that his hands and legs trembled. Rumbles sounded deep in his belly, and he was amazed he had made it through that torturing session without shitting himself. Probably should have asked to use the toilet before he left, but wasn't exactly expecting kindness from his captors.

And now, he was cashless. So there was little hope of relieving that rumbly sensation and the restless legs. Normally, he would just rob somebody to get the cash he needed. But it was barely after sunrise. This wasn't the time to break into anyone's home.

Not to mention the fact that his daylight spell was wearing off. Within a month, he would need enough cash to pay a witch to rejuvenate its power.

That was how it worked for vampires. The sunlight burned like no other. It didn't kill them, but the warm sun on his arms now would be intolerable by the time summer hit.

Realistically, all he needed to feed his habit was a twenty or two. That spell, however? At least five-hundred. No idea how he was going to come up with that. Especially after everyone heard what had just gone down with that Witch and Werewolf.

"You need a ride, man?" someone called from a car to his left.

Nothing too fancy. Not someone he could rob, Oliver feared. Just a little Jetta. The guy inside was put together enough, but he doubted well off. A button up, only buttoned to the middle of his hairy chest, a pair of dark washed blue jeans, a clean shaven jaw, pale blue eyes, and a balding, silvery blonde head.

"You sure?" Oliver asked.

Slowing to a stop, the guy reached across the interior and propped open the passenger side door. "Hop in."

As restless as his legs were, this walk was not treating Oliver's stomach kindly. So, he did as the man asked. Once he was settled in, Oliver thanks the man, who introduced himself as Tyler. While it may not have seemed like the best idea to get in the car of a stranger, Oliver could hold his own in a fight. Could tear a throw it out in the process. He wasn't concerned. Didn't have the strength to tear out of throat at the moment, but if adrenaline kicked in, he would do as he had to.

After asking Oliver which way he was headed, Tyler said, "Not such a warm welcome, huh?"

Oliver's face surely showed his confusion.

"At that girl's house. Brooke, I think her name is," Tyler said. "I've got my eye on the two of them too. Not really sure what I think of them either."

With a harrumph, Oliver took a long drag off his cigarette. "I think she's a real fucking cunt."

"No shit, really?" Tyler asked. "Seems like a nice girl. I've seen her around the bar and everything."

Oliver was not about to open his mouth about what happened inside there. Brooke was terrifying in a way that Oliver had a hard time putting into words, but he believed her when she said she'd kill him. "Spades, you mean?"

"Yeah, nice little place," Tyler said. "Got kicked out of there a while back though. Had a little blow on me, bartender didn't like it, and there went my membership. Said he'd only let me back in on the word of another member. You don't happen to be one, do you?"

Although Oliver knew about Spades, he got a similar message years ago. People like him, vampires, weren't allowed inside. Not without someone to vouch for them. "No, they don't let my kinda people in."

"You know any members who might want to vouch for me?" Tyler asked. "Just a name, even. Maybe a number, or an address. I'd really appreciate it. I can make it worth your while."

That piqued Oliver's interest. Turning to Tyler, Oliver gave a smile. "How much we talking?"

CHAPTER THIRTEEN

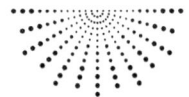

BROOKE

O liver said the place was secluded, and that was putting it mildly. After traffic, it was almost a two-hour drive from my place. Since I lived pretty deep in the city, that didn't say much. Getting stuck in traffic was a common enough occurrence. But even without traffic, it would've taken at least an hour to get there.

We were on Declan's bike. That seemed like the better option. If it were deep in the city, my car would blend in. Out here, though? Declan needed to park deep in the bushes if we wanted to stay off the radar. But even from where he had parked, there was a bit of a walk ahead of us.

The old Victorian stood three stories tall. Although it was probably once a thing of beauty, it was like something out of a horror movie. But not because of whatever creatures lived inside. One of the windows was busted, covered by a piece of plywood. The gutters that still remained were half-fallen off of the roof. I couldn't tell if the siding had once been white, or if it was intended to be gray. It was closer to brown now, covered in a thick layer of dust and soot.

The grass was more than knee-high. An old car with a broken window and two flat tires sat off to the side of the house. Even here, tucked deep in the pines, orange needle caps littered the ground. I imagined there were many more along the overgrown concrete pathway to the house. Beer cans decorated the decrepit porch. Trash bags full of gods only knew what blocked what could have been a nice place to sit with a newspaper and a cup of coffee.

That was the horror show here. Drugs. This house looked the way it did, not because it was home to a Vampire, or Demon, or Witch, or Were-wolf. It looked like shit because the owner was a dealer getting high on his own supply, I imagined.

If Davey and his cohorts, whoever owned this place, were Vampires like Oliver, I didn't understand them. There were much better things to do with a long, immortal life than get high. The number of books I wanted to read would take me at least a dozen lifetimes. Hell, I doubted I would ever get through my to-be-read pile as it was, and that was after narrowing it down to the books that I wanted to read the most. And what were these guys doing with their time?

Not exploring the literary minds of history. Not diving into a new world of wonder every time they opened the pages. Not curing cancer. Not solving the philosophical qualms of life. Not in any way bettering society, or even themselves.

Getting high. As if getting high was good for anyone.

That was the thing I never understood about addiction. Sure, you do the drug for a fun time, and it's great. But then, it's not. It becomes the center of everything. Nothing else matters. There is no life aside from it. I didn't understand with my dad, and I didn't understand it with Ria. It just seemed so silly, so nonsensical, to me. When everything revolved around a drug, around a short-lived rush, what was the point of being alive? Why would anyone want to live that way?

And the kicker was, every time I asked an addict that question, none of them had an answer for me.

And that inability to understand addiction infuriated me.

It infuriated me that—for whatever reason—these fuckers wrecked my house. They dumped a body at Declan's favorite place in the world. And for what? I didn't know them, neither did he, and they wanted to fuck up our lives? They wanted to destroy the life of the person I loved more than anything? What had we done to them?

Did it matter?

No. It didn't.

With a fire under my ass, I stomped closer to the house. At my tail, all but jogging to maintain my speed, Declan called, "We're going in?"

"*We* don't have to," I said, almost at the walkway now. "But I am."

"Well, you're not going in there alone." His tone told me how little he appreciated my approach here. "What's the game plan? We gonna knock?"

"Nope." Almost at the porch now, I veered to the right. There was a window on the porch, but plywood covered its broken frame. I needed a look inside. Winding the bend to the north side of the house, I said, "I'm gonna need a boost."

"A boost for what?" Declan asked.

He'd see.

Finally at the window, I rolled onto the tips of my toes to peek inside. But, as I'd expected, I was a hair too short.

Turning to Declan, I nodded toward the window. "I need that boost."

He furrowed his brows for half a second. Then the obvious realization set in. Letting out a deep breath, a half-smile teased the corners of his lips. "You're gonna break in."

"No breaking."

"But you need to see inside to be able to teleport inside," he said. "Otherwise you'll end up inside a wall or some shit."

"Yep."

"You gonna open the door for me?"

"Obviously."

He arched a brow. "Promise?"

"I promise. Now chop-chop." Clapping my hands, I gestured to the window again. "Give me that boost."

"What's your plan here, Brooke? What're we doing?" he asked. "Gonna sit on the couch 'til the dude gets here?"

"Something like that." I propped my hands on my hips. "Are you gonna help me or not?"

"When you tell me what you're doing."

Grunting, I waved a dismissive hand at him and spun around. A few cinder blocks were stacked at the corner. Looked like my way in. Starting that direction, I said, "If you're not strong enough to lift me up, you could just say so."

He snorted. "You don't listen to a word that comes out of my mouth."

"Well." Squatting to grab the cinder block, grunting, I struggled out, "If you *were* strong enough, you'd just—"

And before I knew it, his hands were on either side of my ribs. They didn't even slide to my armpits as he hoisted me up. Just lifted my nearly three-hundred-pound body clear over his head so I sat on his shoulders, legs outstretched around his neck. There was no stopping the smile that taunted the edges of my lips as he walked back to the window, holding me high enough to see the interior.

His voice was level, not strained in the slightest by my weight. "Keep running that mouth of yours, and I'm gonna shut you up with my dick down your throat."

Fighting that half-smile, I shielded my eyes from the sun and squinted through the glass. "That a threat? Or a promise?"

It was as shitty in there as it was out here. Broken furniture, all dirty and gray. Piles of papers and trash everywhere..

Declan kissed the inside of my knee. "Promise."

I patted his head. "'Atta boy."

He started to say something, probably to call me a bitch, but I'd already teleported inside.

Messy didn't even begin to cover it. The place was littered with needles and bongs and pipes. Maybe the walls were white once, but such a thick layer of soot covered them, I couldn't tell if it was yellow or brown. No pictures hung on them, but a handful of band posters and tapestries did. Burn holes decorated the sofa, the old corduroy recliner, even the throw rug. There may have been a design on it once, but I couldn't make it out now.

It looked like home. Every home I'd lived in when I was growing up had looked like some variation of this place.

When I was a kid, watching my dad nod off on a sofa not much different than this one, I swore to myself that as soon as I was grown, I would never walk into a place like this again. I would get out of this shit. I would have pretty bookshelves, and clean floors, and beautiful knick-knacks. It would always smell like flowers, or apples, or cinnamon, or honey, or anything else. Anything but weed and cigarettes and stale beer.

Yet here I was. Standing in a house exactly like the hell I'd grown up in.

I'd done everything right. I'd gone to school. I'd gotten a good job. I had the pretty bookshelves, and the clean floors, and the nice knickknacks. My house *always* smelled like honey and flowers. But here I was.

The chaos of substance abuse was like a cat, and I was a mouse. No matter how far I ran from it, no matter how careful I was, its claws dug through my flesh all the way to my heart. It stayed there, lodged deep in the muscle that kept me alive, because if I tried to pull away, I'd bleed out. It was all I knew, it was my normal, and there was nothing I wanted more than to escape it, but I was stuck in its claws, and I didn't know how to free myself from that violent grasp.

Declan was already at the door when I swung it open. He said some-thing, but I paid him no mind. *Couldn't* pay him any mind.

There was a baseball bat propped against the wall by the door. Almost thoughtless, I grabbed it.

Before I could even think, I slammed it into a blue bong on the coffee table. Then a clear two-footer on the old, grime covered end table. Then another that stood on the floor.

I smashed the glass of the few framed photos around the room. There weren't people in them, just old artwork, likely purchased at a thrift store. Maybe they were here when they got the house.

I didn't know and I didn't care.

They wrecked my house, so I was wrecking theirs. They wanted to make my life hell? Frame Declan for something he hadn't done? Ruin his life? Rip everything out from under him when he'd never done anything to anyone?

I didn't know for absolute certain that they'd done that part, but I knew my life was fine at this time last week. Then Alicia was murdered and dumped at Declan's, and someone who hung out here trashed my house? There was no way in hell those events weren't connected.

Thrashing the baseball bat into the coffee table, it only shook every-thing that sat on its top. I slammed it down again, and again, and again. The center caved, and everything on its top plummeted to the ground. But I didn't stop there. On the fifth—or maybe tenth—bash, a hand curled around my wrist.

In my ear, Declan said, "You got it, sweetheart. Next hit's gonna drop us into the basement."

Only then, with his breath on my neck and his skin on mine, did I fall from my red-rage haze back into reality. Only then did I see the mess I'd made.

What Oliver did to my place was nothing compared to what I did here.

It was shitty when I had begun, but it was in shambles now. Destroyed. I'd busted every lamp, each piece of furniture aside from the couch and recliner. Even the TV had a hole in its center. I didn't remember doing that, but it felt good to look at.

Maybe the claws of this life were in the center of my heart, but I would thrash and fight like hell to keep my pretty bookshelves, and my nice floors, and my beautiful knickknacks.

Trailing his fingers up my arm slowly, Declan kissed my cheek. "Let's sit down."

1 4

DECLAN

s we sat on the sofa, I searched for the words.

Part of me wanted to hash out what I'd gathered. This place smelled a hell of a lot like Oliver, telling me that Davey—or whoever the hell he really was—likely came from the same race. Vampire. Meaning the fight we were in for when he got home wouldn't last long. Vampires thought they were tough shit, but they stood next to no chance against a Werewolf. Let alone a Werewolf and a Witch, Guardian hybrid.

But that wasn't what I cared about right now.

While I watched Brooke demolish this room, I'd feared for her. I feared for what this meant, because I didn't understand.

What was it about Oliver trashing her house that sent her on this rampage? Sure, nobody wanted something like this to occur, but it had to have been deeper than her messy house. It had to have been deeper than her safety. She took care of Oliver in heartbeats, even made him clean up the house, so what was this about?

Watching her trash this place was like watching a tornado unleashed on a city. She'd tortured a man with precision this morning, but *this* was what sent her over the edge? Why?

Sitting beside her, I watched deep breaths pant in and out of her chest. Her jaw was taut, eyes narrowed, lips curled. Disgusted.

I broke the silence with, "You okay?"

She spared me a glance but continued eyeing the damage. "Yeah. I'm fine."

Gently, as soft as I could be, I found her fingers entwined them between mine. She let me. She didn't pull away, and I was grateful for that. "I mean this with love, sweetheart, but you don't look it."

Typically, she'd tell me to fuck off or something to that effect, but she just stared around the room for a few moments. Eventually, she said, "I just don't get it."

"Why he broke into your house?"

"That too, but no." Her voice was soft, way softer than usual, but she still didn't meet my gaze. "This life."

When I said nothing, waiting for her to continue, still struggling to understand, she only gave me another glance. That anger in her eyes was gone now, replaced by something I'd never seen on Brooke's face. A feeling that bubbled deep inside her and poured out onto me. Although I made no attempt to read her mind, I felt what she did. And it hit me like a ten ton truck.

Pain, sure, but it was a certain type of pain. One I'd never felt as deeply as I did until this moment.

Betrayal. She felt betrayed.

"It's poetic, isn't it? My whole life, I've dealt with the shit, but I've never been in it. I smoked weed a couple times, I drink on occasion, but I've never been *engulfed* in this life. And this is always where I end up. It's how it works. Addicts, they don't care. Some of us do our damnedest to rise above this bullshit, but somehow, they still weasel their way in. They find a way to fuck up everything that somebody else cares about. This isn't my fucking problem, but here I am. Just like it wasn't my problem when Dad couldn't keep the shit together, and I had to take care of Ria, or when I had to clean up the needles he left on the floor, or when I had to make myself dinner even though I couldn't reach the stove, and it's bullshit. It's just such fucking bullshit that no matter how hard I tried to get away from the ship, this is where I fucking end up."

Wow. She talked about something. She shared something with me. Something deep and personal.

Granted, she did it in a relatively aggressive, pissed off way, but she did, in fact, share something with me.

No matter how much I appreciated it, I wasn't sure how to respond to it. I didn't understand the way she felt either. Why did she feel betrayed? I could've asked, but I wasn't sure if she even wanted me to respond. Maybe she just wanted me to listen. And if, for once, she wanted to let me know how she felt, she wanted to share, I wasn't gonna push for more. I'd wait for it.

So, that was all he did. I listened, and I held her hand.

Quietly, almost too quiet for me to hear, she finally met my gaze and whispered, "Are we thinking the same thing?"

All I was thinking was that I was grateful she allowed me an ounce of vulnerability. "What are you thinking?"

"Neither of us do drugs. Then two days ago, an addict was murdered and left behind your bar. Today, an addict broke into my house and trashed it." With a hard swallow, I swore I felt her hand tremble. "But, the two of us, we both know an addict."

And it clicked.

That's where the betrayal came from. Someone she'd given everything to, someone she'd fought so hard to protect all her life, was linked to this. Setting me up, starting a storm between me and Brooke, murdering an innocent woman...

The only connection here was the one person Brooke would do anything for. Ria.

I opened my mouth to respond—to tell her we didn't know that for sure—but the squeal of door hinges cut me off.

Brooke disappeared.

A thump, then a gag, sounded from the front door. Pain ached through my stomach, as though I had been elbowed in the ribs. But it wasn't me. It wasn't my pain that I felt.

I ran to the entryway. Just in time to see a large man—white, around my height, and on the heavier side—body slam Brooke backwards into a wall. Same thing I would've done if some random person appeared in my house with a blade pressed to my throat from behind, as Brooke had.

But no way in hell I could let that fly.

Suddenly, it was a blur of punches and fists and thrashes and pain. A lot of pain, but most of it was blurred by the adrenaline.

In my peripheral, I saw that Brooke was on the ground. That was okay, because I had the guy pressed against the wall with a hand around his throat. That only lasted for half a second. He dropped a fist into my gut, just enough for me to release my hold.

Then I was up against the wall. His fist connected with my face again, and again, and again. Stars shined against my eyes, throbbing through the back of my head.

Then, her voice carried. I couldn't make out the words, but I knew what she was doing. My greatest strength was this. Brute force. Hers were spells.

The man before me groaned in misery. Blood dribbled from the corners of his eyes, trailing down his face. He stumbled backwards, releasing me. Screaming at the top of his lungs, he grasped the banister of the stairs for support. "Stop! Sucking stop!"

Brooke did.

Wiping some blood from the corner of my lip, I breathed hard. Already, the pain was disintegrating, my body healing. He stared at me, the best he could through the blood, and I stared at him, and when he glanced at Brooke, I snapped, "Put your hands on her again. I dare you."

He sniffed a few times, eyes still leveled on me. "Nah, I don't need to. I think I made my point this morning."

And there it was.

"Why?" Staggering to her feet, Brooke harrumphed. "Why are you doing this, Davey? I'm assuming, at least. That's what the little bastard you sent to my house called you."

Giving a half smile, lifting the bottom of his shirt to his eyes, he wiped away the remaining streams of blood. "Things'll die down. We both know you're not going away for this. I didn't frame you."

"No, just wanted to make our lives hell for a while," I snapped. "Answer her fucking question. Why are you doing this?"

"Why do you think?" Laughing, he narrowed his eyes at Brooke. "Ask your sister."

Slowly, heartache washed through Brooke's expression.

God damn it.

Still holding the banister, with his free hand, Davey slipped the decorative ornament on its spindle off. He snatched something from inside.

And, like that, the door swung open. A gust of wind tossed it us through it.

CHAPTER FIFTEEN

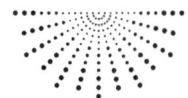

DECLAN

The brunt of my bodyweight slammed to the soil with a thundering *thwack*. But Brooke? She'd disappeared midflight. Could she have extended me the same courtesy? Teleported me, so I didn't fall flat on my ass? Yes, she could've. Had she? No. Of course not.

A *ring-ring* sounded in my pocket. After struggling onto my ass, I flicked it open. A text from Emory flashed across the screen.

Tyler's here. He wants to talk to Brooke. He's waiting outside until she shows. I called her, but it went to voicemail. I figured she's with you.

"Great," I said under my breath, still struggling upright. Although I was healing, my ass hurt like a mother.

"What is it?" Brooke asked. By the time I was finding my footing, she was reading over my shoulder.

Like she hadn't helped me to keep from landing how I had, I didn't help her by extending the phone. Just snapped it shut, stowed it to my pocket, and started to my bike.

"Seriously?" Brooke called out behind me. "What—you gonna leave me here?"

"When have I ever left you behind?" Spinning toward her, I made no attempt to lower my voice. "When have I ever intentionally said or done something I knew would hurt you? When, Brooke?"

Unlike I'd expected, she swallowed hard. Like she couldn't fathom why it bothered me that she couldn't do me the smallest service of teleporting me so I didn't land in misery after the bomb that'd just been dropped on us.

And as much as I wanted to stay angry, when I looked at her, that became harder than the last few days had been. There was something in her eyes I couldn't quite describe. They were soft, gentle even, like a retired pit bull who'd lived its life in dog fighting rings and now feared for its life in a good home.

God damn it. I wasn't trying to hurt her—sure as shit wasn't trying to scare her—but God fucking damn it. I wasn't happy. As, honestly, I felt I had the right to be.

"We can't—" Her voice cracked, and she stopped to clear it away. "We can't talk about what just happened?"

"Not here." Stepping over the bike, I nodded to her seat in the back. "Not now. Let's go."

Again, unlike how I'd expected her to respond, she simply... did.

She climbed onto the back of the bike behind me. As she got situated, fastening her helmet around her head, I watched her fumble with her hands in the side mirror. Normally, she rode with her hands around my waist or resting on my thighs. That was the best way to stay balanced on a bike, especially because I didn't have a sissy bar.

Jesus Christ. I wanted to be mad—I *was* mad—but not that mad. Not so mad I wanted her to feel like she couldn't touch me. Like I hated her.

I didn't. I doubted I ever could.

This wasn't her fault. I knew that. I didn't blame her, not entirely. But I was hurt. Not even by Brooke, but Ria. Pain in the ass or not, I loved the little brat.

I was just angry. I didn't want Brooke to think I was done with her, as I was sure that was the reason for the face she'd given me a moment prior. Afraid that her crazy family would be my last straw. That it was over now.

Her family was a shit show. I had known so days into our meeting. It wasn't Brooke's fault Ria was an addict, caught up in whatever the hell all this was. Honestly, given the way they'd grown up, I couldn't even say it was Ria's fault.

I didn't know that yet. I didn't have the full story, and I needed it before I did or said anything else.

But regardless of what I learned, Brooke wouldn't be the one I blamed.

I took her hands and pulled them around my waist. "Stay close, alright?" I said, softening my tone.

All she did was nod against my back.

Turning over the engine, flicking up the kickstand, with her body so close to mine now, I was certain of that look. The scent of fear—cortisol mixed with adrenaline—filled my nose.

I wanted to tell her she didn't have anything to be afraid of. But since we were heading to see a cop that she'd have to lie to about all this? Yeah, there was definitely something to fear.

———

Just as Emory said he'd be, Tyler stood against his black cruiser when we rolled in on the bike. Suit and tie finely pressed, neat hair was slicked back from his face. Even though he smiled, it was strained. Quite literally, like he had a stick up his ass. That phrase never made much sense to me, but now, looking at Tyler, that was the only way to describe that smile. Like he had a stick shoved up his ass and hated how much he liked it.

No sooner than Brooke had dismounted did the interrogation begin. "You must be Brooke," he said, walking closer. "Sorry I missed you yesterday."

"Yeah, he was too busy harassing me." I made no effort to say so subtly.

"Aw, baby, be nice." Running a hand down my chest, Brooke's entire demeanor changed.

Her usual fast, blunt words fell from her lips smoother than silk. That little white sundress she'd thrown on this morning, the one I'd seen as sexier than sin on her just after she'd begged and whimpered for me to lick her pussy, only to torture a man half to death, suddenly looked so dainty. Even the way she held herself had changed. While she typically stood firm, strong, all of her limbs were looser now. Delicate. I'd never put "Brooke" and "delicate" in the same sentence, but that was the only word I could use for her now. The octave of her voice even heightened. Like she was doing everything in her power to appear as a different person. No denying the work she put in to dip her chest, too, when she extended her hand. She had to crouch to reach the son of a bitch, but she somehow managed to show off every inch of cleavage when she did.

"He's just doing his job. Isn't that right, Detective...?"

"Tyler." Bastard let his gaze linger there for far too long. If the situation were any different, I'd run my mouth about it. But this was Brooke's plan evidently. Seduce the guy into leaving us alone. "Detective Grant Tyler."

"Oh, that's right." She giggled. Brooke could giggle? Why the fuck had she never laughed like that for me before? "Emory said so when he called, but it completely slipped my mind."

"Happy to meet you." Still shaking her hand, still eyeing her tits, Tyler stayed silent for a few heartbeats. It was only when I cleared my throat that he met her gaze. "Well, I wish it were under better circumstances."

"Oh, of course." One of her hands found my arm, but with the other, Brooke fingered the necklace that hung just above her breasts. And yes, I said *fingered* because it was beyond intentionally drawing his attention back there. She traced her fingers over her cleavage softly. It was subtle enough that it didn't look like a porno, like she was holding her hand over her heart in shock, but I could see what she was doing. "We were so devastated to hear about Alicia. Whoever did this orphaned two kids under three, did you know that? Just horrible."

Sociopath. My girlfriend was a fucking sociopath.

"Yeah," Tyler said, his gaze shifting to me. "Whoever did this is a damn monster."

"Jesus fucking Christ." I dropped my jacket onto the back of my bike. "I told you a thousand times. I never met the girl. I sure as shit didn't kill her."

"Oh, God, no." Clenching my bicep, Brooke's eyes grew softer than I'd yet seen them. "He couldn't have, sir. He was with me all night."

"Yeah, that's what he said." Tyler eyed me up and down for a moment before turning back to Brooke. "You willing to put that in writing?"

"Oh, of course." Tracing her fingers up and down my arm, her voice remained soft. "Really, he was with me every moment. He went to the bathroom once or twice, but he never left the bar. There's no way he would've had time to hurt anyone. Well, I think anyway. Do you know what time it was when Alicia... Well, you know." Innocent. Her voice, her demeanor, everything about her was so innocent all of a sudden. "Has the —Oh, gosh, what's the name? Colander? You know, that doctor who takes care of people once they've passed."

"Coroner?" Tyler asked.

Not only was she playing the sweet and innocent girl, but the clueless one too. Brooke was many things, but stupid wasn't one of them. The girl practically studied the Oxford Dictionary.

"Right. That's it. The coroner." She chuckled, tapping herself on the head. "Has the coroner figured out what time she passed? They can do that, can't they? I think I saw that on TV before."

"Yes, sweetheart, they can," Tyler said.

I had to lock up all my limbs to keep from shifting. Nobody called her sweetheart but me.

"That poor woman. She wasn't out here for long, was she?"

Sparing me a glance before leveling again on Brooke, Tyler shook his head. "Not long at all, no."

"Oh God, that just makes it worse." With a deep frown, Brooke held me closer. "If we would've been out here, maybe we could've helped."

"Well, it looks like a dump site." The moment those words left Tyler's lips, his mouth dropped. Although he recovered, he knew that evidence would destroy his case against me, and he wasn't sure why he had said it aloud. He cleared his throat. "I don't think you should blame yourself, is all."

"Goodness," Brooke murmured, fingering her necklace again. "Well, as awful as it is, it couldn't have been Declan then, right? He doesn't have a car."

"Do you?"

"Have a car? Oh, sure. Do you wanna take a look at it?" Still so innocent. Still so sweet. "I don't mind. I could bring it down to the station tomorrow. It's back at my house though."

"If you could bring it down to the station tomorrow"—Tyler held out his business card—"when you give your statement, I'd really appreciate it."

"Sure thing, Detective." A soft, solemn smile. "Thank you so much for your service."

He returned the smile, then shot me a glare. "Right. I'll see you two soon."

"Hopefully under better circumstances," Brooke said.

Tyler let out an odd little huff of a laugh. "Hopefully," was all he said before returning to his car.

As Tyler stepped inside the vehicle and closed his door, Brooke's hold on my arm loosened. She waited until he was out of sight, driving down the road, barely a blur on the spring brightened highway, to release me. Taking a step back, she propped her hands on her hips. There was still a certain softness in her eyes, but I couldn't call her dainty anymore. "Can we talk?"

"Yeah. Let's talk about how you're fucking crazy."

Face screwing up in some combination of pain and annoyance, she harrumphed. "Excuse me?"

I couldn't even find the words. All I did, all I could do, was shake my head and walk away.

Close behind me, she called, "How am I crazy? What did I do?"

"Seriously? You gonna act like that was normal, Brooke?"

"What are you talking about?" She was only a foot or two behind me when I reached the door. Normally, I would have held it open for her. Today, I didn't have the patience.

"Declan. I thought you said we were going to talk. Are we not? You're just going to storm off?"

"Storm off?" Over my shoulder, I shot her glare and continued around the bar. "How the fuck do you do that?"

"How the fuck do I do what?"

Grabbing a bottle of whiskey from the back shelf, not so much as waving to Emory in greeting, I poured myself a large glass. "Act like a whole other god damned person. One second, you're a raging bitch, and the next, you're playing dumb blonde? Like you don't know exactly what's going on here?"

"I *don't* know what's going on here," she snapped. "And I was just doing what I had to. Yeah, I pretended to be sweet and innocent, because that's what works. Cops like dumb girls." She stood on the other side of the bar, grasping either end of it and leaning in. Her eyes were full of fire. Her voice was no different. "What did you want me to do? I did what I fucking had to. You're gonna call me crazy for that? Act like I'm a horrible person? Like I did something wrong, when I probably just saved your fucking ass?"

"After your sister put it on the god damn fire!" I wanted to scream something else, not giving a flying fuck about all the patrons turning our way. But I chugged the whiskey instead and lowered my voice. "Ria did this. You know that. Don't act like you're stupid, Brooke. Might work on a dumb cop, but it doesn't work on me. Your little sister had something to do with that girl's murder, had something to do with that Vampire breaking in your house, and you're arguing with me? Like I'm the villain here?"

"I'm arguing with you because you called me fucking crazy—"

"I called you crazy because no sane person could act the way that you just fucking acted. Psychopaths, that's who act the way that you just did. Great show, by the way. You should win a fucking Oscar for that."

"Hang on," she said, letting out a strained laugh. "You're mad because

I manipulated a cop. Seriously? I'm sorry. I'm sorry that my life wasn't as cushy as yours. I'm sorry that I had to learn how to do that to survive. I'm sorry that I worked for the Chambers, and they *taught* me how to do that. I'm sorry that I'm not a little damsel in distress you have to rescue."

"I swear, you're the most emotionally inept woman I have ever met in my life." Laughing, I shook my head. "You really don't see what I'm upset about. You really don't get it at all. You always think it comes down to some feminist issue, and it never fucking does, Brooke. It's always about *you*. You, being a fucking angel to everyone else, and a raging cunt to me."

Mouth dropping in disbelief, she shook her head. "How was I being a cunt today? What'd I do? What was so bad that justifies the way you're talking to me right now?"

"Almost two years together," I snapped. "Two god damned years, and not once have you shown me an ounce of vulnerability."

"Two nights ago, a body was found outside of your bar. A woman was murdered, and this is what you're worried about? My emotional vulnerability, that's your concern?! Calling me crazy, telling me that I'm a psychopath, that's your priority at the moment. Not, I don't know, the living nightmare that's raining down around us?!" She was yelling now, too, and everyone in the bar had turned to see.

Granted, it was early. There were only half a dozen people here, and most of them had seen something like this before, but I wasn't in the mood to fight. I wasn't in the mood for any of this shit.

She kept yelling though, and I started walking away. "This has nothing to do with me, and you know it. You're just mad, you're taking it out on me, and that's not fair—"

"You know what's not fair?!" I spun to face her, nearly at the hall toward the office now. "The fact that I tell you I love you every single day, and you haven't said it to me once."

Eyes wide, she shook her head. "That's not true. You know I do. I tell you how much you mean to me all the time—"

"So now you're going to try and make me think that I'm crazy?!" I gestured toward Emory at the other end of the bar. "Him and your sister have a bet. How much money is on it, I don't know, but they had a bet on how long it'd take me to notice. Not once, Brooke. You haven't told me you love me *one single time*."

"That's not true—"

"Then say it!" I flung my arms up. "Say it right now. Say, 'I love you, Declan.' Just fucking say it."

Laughing again, she shook her head. "I can't believe you think that I don't love you."

"Then why can't you say it?"

Her mouth opened. No words came out. It lifted up and down, as if she just couldn't form the words. Because she didn't feel them, she couldn't make them.

"That's what I thought." I turned back around. And suddenly, she was in front of me.

With her hands on my chest, face still screwed up in that combination of annoyance and pain, she shook her head. "I do. *I do.* I swear, I do."

"Then why can't you say it?"

Shaking her head again, I swore, for half a second, there were tears in those eyes. And I almost felt guilty. Like this was somehow my fault. Like I hadn't gotten to this point because time and time again, she had made me feel like I didn't matter. Like our life together, if we even had one, didn't matter.

Then again, what life together? She was the biggest part of mine, and I was northing more than a speck in hers.

"Because you won't let me in. Because the moment there is an opportunity to show an ounce of vulnerability, you shove it away. God forbid you have feelings. God forbid you care about somebody. I've shown you not once, not twice, but a thousand times, how much you mean to me. I've been there for you through any and everything. And you can't even tell me you love me? Because you don't. You fucking don't, Brooke. I don't matter to you. You're stuck with me because of the soulmate shit, so you deal with me, but you don't fucking want me."

I was sure this time. There were tears in her eyes.

"That's not true."

"Bullshit," I snapped. "Fucking bullshit."

Spinning around again, I started toward the back door. It was the quickest way to get to my house behind the bar. And I was really hoping she would stay where she was, but she was right behind me.

"Declan, stop it." Her voice trembled. And I hated that it made my chest warm. Not because I wanted her to be in pain, but because that may have been the first time since I met her that she showed me an ounce of emotion, that she showed me that she actually cared whether I stayed or went. That the possibility of losing me, that watching me walk away, hurt.

Really, hurting her was the last thing I wanted. But, god damn it, I was tired of bashing my head off the wall. I was tired of giving her everything in this relationship and getting nothing for it. I wanted her attention, good or bad. I wanted to see her feel something, *anything*, for me. Because after that performance with Tyler, I was convinced she didn't. I was convinced none of it had been real.

She kept calling out to me, but I didn't say a word. Not until we were at the door, and she said, "What am I doing wrong?"

In a trembling voice yanking open the door, I shot her a look over my shoulder. "I just told you."

"I'm with you every day," she said, lifting her hands to either side of her head and grabbing fistfuls of hair. "I make you dinner. I see something at the store that reminds me of you, and I get it. I fight with you, I know that, but you do it, too. You're doing it right now. I'm not perfect, and I've never claimed to be, but you're the center of my world, Declan. Outside of my job, and Ria, you are all I have. You're the only one who sticks around, the only one I can count on, and I try to be that for you, too." Her voice cracked again. "Am I not? Am I not what you want? Am I not what you need? What am I doing wrong? Because I don't understand. I don't understand, Declan. I don't know what else I can do. I don't know how to show you how much you mean to me."

"An ounce of vulnerability. Just a fucking drop, Brooke. Tell me what's going on in your head. Don't make me break into your mind to see it. Talk to me. Fucking communicate. For once, just once, act like I mean as much to you as you do to me. Because the only time I feel like I even matter is when I'm fucking you. That's the only time you show me the slightest bit of fucking vulnerability."

She laughed again, but this one was more genuine and less sarcastic. "And since when has that been a problem for you? Last time I checked, you're the one who initiates ninety-nine percent of the time. You're the one who starts fights with me just so you can rail me, and now what? You're going to make me feel like a dirty slut for that? Because I like fucking you? In case you forgot, that's how our relationship started—"

"And that's the only time you let your walls down." We were in the threshold now, the door still open behind her. Only a foot or two apart, I wagged my finger in her face. "I wasn't calling you a slut. If you want me to, I will. You know I will. But don't spin this around into something that it isn't. I'm not shaming you for a god damned thing aside from your emotionally unavailability."

"What do you want me to do? Write you a fucking sonnet? Scream from the rooftops that you mean everything to me?" Turning back out the door, she yelled, "I may be emotionally unavailable, but apparently, I'm great in the sack! Apparently, that's all I give Declan! Just so everybody knows!"

"Are you five?" I asked. "We can't have a serious conversation without you —"

"And I'm crazy!" she yelled. "I'm a psychopath! Or maybe, sociopath." She turned back to look at me. "Which one was it again?" She turned back outside. "It doesn't matter. Apparently, Declan is the perfect one in this relationship, and I'm a failure! I'm a failure for saving his ass, and sucking his dick like a champ, and doing everything—"

Grabbing her by the waist and hauling her away from the door, I slammed it shut. "I can't stand you."

"Somehow, I'm the bad guy," she said.

Backing her into the wall, I took her face in my hand. "I said you were crazy. I didn't say you were the bad guy."

"You haven't seen me crazy." An impossible fire flashed through her eyes. "Even today. I wasn't crazy, Declan. Call me a bitch if you want to, but I'm not crazy. I'm independent, and I'm a cunt, and you *love* to hate that. You hate that I don't need you. My life has been more fucked up than yours, and I had to learn shit you never had to. If I didn't, we wouldn't have fucking survived. That's what you hate. You hate that I can do things without you. But I don't need —"

Grabbing her face, I leaned in and kissed her hard. So hard that I felt the ache of the wall against her back. Lifting her up around my hips, kissing her, grinding my hips against hers, hearing her whimper, I grabbed a fistful of her hair and yanked her head back.

The smell of her arousal drifted into my nostrils, and I ground in closer, relishing in the little whimper she released. "Oh, you don't need me? Not for anything, huh?"

CHAPTER SIXTEEN

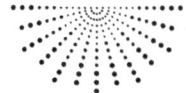

Brooke

One moment, he was kissing me, pinning me to the wall with his body, and the next, I was shoving him up against the opposite wall in the hallway, tearing off his shirt. Then my panties were on the floor, and his jeans weren't far behind, and he was lifting me into the air again, only to set me down on the entry table. Everything on its top was clattering to the floor, but all he cared about was unhooking my bra.

With each touch of our lips, I couldn't tell if we were trying to tongue fuck one another's mouths, or if we were trying to tear each other faces off. When I pulled away for half a second, and he bit my lip to keep me where he wanted me, I had to assume the latter.

This made no sense. We made no sense.

I knew that. Clearly, so did he. That's why we were here. That's why this was happening the way it was, the way it so often did.

I loved him. Whether he knew it or not, whether he believed me or not, I fucking loved him. If I didn't, I wouldn't have let him manhandle me into his bedroom and toss me onto the bed like some sort of toy.

For him, I would be that. If he asked me to lie there like a fuck doll, I would. If he wanted me to suck his dick while he watched a football game, not paying me an ounce of mind otherwise, I would. Whatever he wanted, sexually or any other context, I would give it to him.

Any time he needed me, anytime he wanted me, I was there. I may have been there with an attitude, but I was there. I was always there to give him what he needed, to be there however he needed me to be, and I didn't know what more I had to do to prove it to him.

And it infuriated me. It infuriated me that I would do anything for this fucking man, and he still didn't believe me when I told him how much he mattered. When I showed him every God damned day.

The fact of it was, he loved my attitude. If he didn't love these fights, he wouldn't start them.

But he did. He always did.

I knew that I wasn't perfect. Never once had I tried to hide that fact. But I hated more than anything that throughout this fight, he made it out like I was the only one with the problem. He treated me as though he was oh-so-much softer than I was. Like he was a big, affectionate teddy bear, and I was a lunatic with a pitchfork.

He wanted to act like I was a horrible bitch? I'd show him one.

When he collapsed to the bed on top of me, bringing his lips to mine once more, I caught his bottom lip between my teeth. Not a gentle nibble, but a bite so hard that I tasted iron on my tongue.

Grabbing my wrists, he pinned me to the bed. Only then did I release his lips.

Declan straightened above me, teeth gritted to a hard line. "Really, Brooke?"

I laughed. Maybe not the smartest thing to do with all things considered, but he looked cute with the blood dribbling from his lip. So angry, so furious, and it was nice to see that I wasn't alone in my misery. "Maybe you're right. Maybe I do need you for one thing."

"And you think a good way to fucking get it is to bite me?" Glaring down at me, he ground his hips and closer, teasing me with the head of his cock. "You're on thin ice, sweetheart. You might want to watch the way you fucking behave right now."

"Why is that?" There was no denying how condescending my voice came off. I didn't care, either. Maybe it was a part of the game. This twisted, sick game of love and romance that the two of us played like a gambler at a slot machine with a credit card that would never run out. "You gonna spank me? Make me bleed? Not much of a punishment if I like it, is it?"

Teeth still gritted, eyes still narrowed, he squeezed my wrists tighter. He squeezed so tight that it hurt. Not just an ache, but a deep, throbbing hurt. But he must've felt it, because as soon as that intense, rumbling pain stretched up my arm, he released. Not entirely, of course. He still had me pinned to the bed, but his grip wasn't so ferocious.

"Oh, no, I know better than that." He swung my arms overhead, then held them in place with one hand. Reaching past me to the corner of the bed, the whoosh of the nylon strap against the silk sheets sounded. He freed one of my arms, tucked a leather cuff around it, then wound it tight. Tighter than usual, but he still checked to make sure that he could slide 2 fingertips between my skin and the cuff. Angry or not, kink was only fun if it was safe. He repeated the process with my other wrist. Once they were bound and secured to the bed, he reached into the nightstand. The buzz of my vibrator sounded a second later. Bringing it to my clit, he gave a wicked smile. "But I know exactly how to punish your bad little ass. You're going to hate every sucking minute of it."

Gasping at the pleasure that quaked through me, I laughed. "Well, I'm not hating it right now."

He grabbed my leg, lifted it onto his shoulder, and plunged deep into me. Didn't take the vibrator off my clit for a second. He pounded so hard into me that I had no doubt he hit my cervix. Hell, he may have been halfway up my intestines. And as much as I wanted to hate it, paired with the power of the vibrations against my clit, I was already moments from a climax.

Hearing the octave of my moan change, knowing I was getting closer, he pulled the vibrator away. I whimpered. He gave me that devious smile again. "Yeah. You're gonna fucking hate this."

Ah, fuck.

Yeah, I was gonna hate this.

Edging's all fun and game's until someone's very mad, and then it's not even close to fucking fun.

"Declan—"

He brought the vibrator back to my clit, slamming his cock into me again. "I'm trying so fucking hard to make this work with you." Pushing the vibe in harder, thrusting so deep that I squealed, he grabbed hold of my face. "But I don't know what the fuck to do with you, Brooke. I'm so god damned tired of fighting with you all the time."

I tried to speak, but he had my face pinched between his thumb and forefingers, so only gibberish came out.

"What was that?" As kind as that sentence may have read, he was still talking through gritted teeth. He released my face just enough to let me try again.

"I didn't start this fight," I made out, squirming beneath his touch.

That pissed him off, because he pumped in harder, slamming an open palm across my tit. I whimpered. He didn't care. "This fight's been brewing for a long time, and we both fucking know it."

No, I didn't.

This was how we were, how we always had been. Was this fight more volatile than the rest? Sure. We usually had attitudes, but we didn't scream at each other. Not the way we just had.

This was the first time it was about us. Most of our fights—no matter how frequent—were about dumb shit. His inability to take off his dirty boots before he walked on my nice rugs. My inability to let him pay when the check came. How I emasculated him by calling him a sourpuss when he showed with an attitude, or how much of a bitch I was with him on a bad day.

This one was different, and no, I hadn't seen it coming.

"And if we're not gonna talk it out like fucking adults, this is what you're gonna get." He pushed the vibrator in deeper, covering my mouth when I screamed that it was too much. If it was really too much, I'd say so in his mind, and he'd stop. But I hadn't reached that point, and he knew it. "You're gonna listen. For once in your life, you're gonna listen to me, damn it."

I'm listening, asshole, I said to his mind.

Jaw tight, he clicked the button, and the intensity of the vibrations picked up.

I yanked desperately against the restraints to no success. Half out of instinct, half because, holy shit, it was too much.

So much that he pulled it away before I could finish.

I whimpered.

"Oh, does that piss you off?" Pulling out of me, releasing my face, he slammed an open palm against my clit. I squealed in a combination of pain and pleasure. "Good. Now you know what it feels like. Now you know what it's like when I say 'I love you,' and you say, 'you too.'"

The passion, the fury of this moment, dissipated. I couldn't help my laugh. "Really? You're gonna do this right now?"

Another open handed slap against my clit.

I squealed that time, and he got way too much fucking joy from it, judging by the release of his jaw.

"Yeah, I fucking am." He thrusted into me again. "The is the only place you let your fucking walls down. Maybe you'll say it back between begging me to let you come."

"Jesus Christ." Scoffing, I shook my head. "You realize how ridiculous you are, right? You tie me to your bed and edge me to get me to profess my love for you?"

He brought the vibrator back to my clit. "Still not an 'I love you.'"

Jolting at the sudden touch or not, I couldn't keep in my laugh. "This is pathetic."

It wasn't fury that flashed through his eyes that time. Hurt did. The slightest pull in his brows, the vaguest downturn of his lips. It vanished as quick as it'd come, and still, the moment I saw that look, I knew I shouldn't have said that.

Not because I cared about the punishment that came next. Not because I hated him edging me for the next hour, or two, or four, if that's how long he kept this going for—and he had before.

Because hurting him hadn't been my intention.

Truthfully, I wasn't sure why that sentence left my lips. Was it true? Yeah, it was. A word, one stupid word, carrying so much relevance was pathetic. But not in the way he was thinking. Of course, I was the one who made him feel that way, and I'd take responsibility for that, but I hadn't said that because I thought he was pathetic. He was anything but.

The weight that word carried for me. That's what was pathetic.

But it didn't matter.

It was too late to take it back.

He was already unclipping the eyehooks on the cuffs and dropping the still buzzing vibrator to the bed.

"Decan—"

"Shut the fuck up." No more fury in his voice. No more anger. Cold, blunt rage instead. "Keep your fucking mouth shut, Brooke."

"But—"

He clasped a hand over my mouth. Eyes like fire burned into mine. "Shut. The. Fuck. Up."

I gulped. Maybe that sounded dramatic, but it wasn't because I was afraid. Not of him, at least. He wouldn't hurt me, not in a physical way that'd cause any lasting damage.

I was afraid of what that meant. What my words meant. The damage I just did to him, to this relationship, that I was afraid I wouldn't be able to undo.

After reaching into the side table again, he came back with a ball gag.

We'd only used that once before. He said he didn't like gagging me because I looked prettier without it. And because he usually liked my smart ass mouth. Supposed I pushed him over the edge this time because he shoved it between my lips and fastened it tight behind my head.

Everything whirred in an almost indistinguishable blur as he yanked me to my feet and brought me to the corner of the room. The corner where a hook hung from the ceiling. As soon as he brought me to my feet, I should've known that was where he was taking me. Aside from over his knee, it was the best place he had to beat my ass.

And as soon as he fastened my wrists to that hook, spread my legs apart, and bent me forward with that vibrator pressed against my clit, that was exactly what he did. A heavy handed smack echoed off my ass. Thrusting into me this time, he planted another, and then another, and another. Didn't pull the vibrator away once though.

"You're everything to me," he said in my ear. There was just the slightest hint of emotion in his voice. I couldn't tell if it was anger or pain. One way or the other, I deserved the next smack. I wasn't so sure I deserved the pleasure of his cock thudding against my g-spot, nor the vibrator, however. "And maybe that is pathetic. Maybe I am."

I tried to shake my head, but he pushed it in deeper, then slapped my ass again.

"Loving someone who doesn't love you back, that is fucking pathetic." Defeat? Was that defeat I heard in his voice?

That wasn't what I—

"Jesus, shut the fuck up, Brooke." Thrusting in again, he pushed the head of that vibrator deep into my clit. So much pressure, so much sensation, paired with so much pain. Physically, sure, but most of it was in my chest. Because I knew I was ruining this, and I didn't know how to fix it. "But I don't know how much longer I can do it for."

Tears budded in my eyes, and I wanted to scream. I wanted to sob. But the pleasure, the undeniable pleasure of his dick, the vibrator on my clit, was too much. It was the most confusing sensation of my life, and maybe because he was right.

This was the only place I allowed myself to feel anything. The only place I let the walls come down. And I hated it. I didn't know how to stop it.

But this wasn't the kind of emotion I wanted to feel. It certainly wasn't the type of pain I liked to mix with pleasure.

"I'm hanging"—thrust—"onto"—thrust—"you"—thrust—"by"—

thrust— "a fucking"—thrust—"thread,"—thrust— "and I need you"—a slow, gentle grind, and a kiss on my neck, before another hard thrust— "to love me back." One more soft, slow kiss on my neck. Still holding that vibrator on my clit, he curled an arm around my waist and hauled me into his chest.

Shutting my eyes, I tried desperately to keep the tears inside.

He pressed the button on the vibe. Again, its intensity picked up. He went back to thrusting, but slower, softer, than he had a moment ago. For a moment, with his arms around me, when he was giving me the pleasure instead of threatening me with it, I thought it was okay. That he wasn't so angry. That we were okay.

And the climax came.

Trembling, falling into his chest, shaking when darkness took hold of my vision, I groaned around the gag. The pleasure overtook me full throttle, peaked by the heat of his cum, the contractions of his cock. I'd had a thousand magnificent orgasms with Declan, but never one like this. Never one so intimate, so vulnerable.

And before mine had even ended, he whispered, "Because I'm gonna walk away, sweetheart. I love you, and I don't want to, but you're not giving me much of a choice."

Only then did it end.

When he felt the contractions slow, he tossed the vibrator onto the bed.

Reaching above me, he released the cuffs.

But when he stepped in front of me, it was almost impossible to meet his gaze. Tears pearled down my cheeks, and I hoped I could pass them off as an involuntary reaction to the pain.

Unbuckling the gag around my face with one hand, he swept a tear away with the other. As it clattered to the ground, he took my face in his hand. "Say it, Brooke. Please say it."

But I couldn't.

I just... couldn't.

So I stood there. Naked, warring with tears in my eyes, staring at him, and trying so hard to form the words, but to no success.

Gradually, any hope that shined in his eyes faded.

He released my cheek, and he walked away.

CHAPTER SEVENTEEN

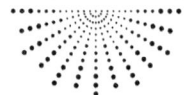

BROOKE

I was already teary-eyed when I was leaving Declan's. I felt like there was a twenty-pound weight sitting on my chest. Everything he said, the way I had apparently made him feel, my never-ending failure to be enough for those around me, it was all weighing on my psyche in a way that it never had before.

I wasn't enough.

That's what it all came down to. I wasn't enough. I wasn't good enough. I wasn't good enough for Declan. I wasn't who he needed in a partner. And I wasn't good enough for my sister.

That's why Ria wound up the way she did. Yeah, I turned out alright. Went to college, got a good job, had the pretty floors, and the nice bookshelves, and the cute knickknacks, and my house always smelled good, but for everyone else, I was a failure. I tried to help, I tried to be what they needed, and my attempts crashed and burned every time.

So imagine my anguish when I landed in my bedroom, only to find my sister digging through my closet. Not on top, where I hung my clothes, or even the shelf overhead where I tucked my bed linens.

On the floor. Where I kept my safe.

There wasn't much in it. A few nice pieces of jewelry, none of which were worth more than a few hundred bucks, and a small nest egg. The money I had left from when I had worked for the Chambers. Barely more than five grand. I didn't trust banks, and it wasn't enough to invest in anything, so that was where I kept it. In case I ever needed to run, in case anyone ever came after me, I had those five thousand dollars tucked in my safe.

And that was what my sister was holding now.

Mouth dropping open when she turned my way, her fingers trembled around the wads of cash.

"Nice," I said. "Just gave you money yesterday, and you're gonna steal from me?"

"It's not—"

"What it looks like?" Swinging my jacket onto the bed, I raked a hand through my hair. "Of course it's not what it looks like. It's never what it looks like, right? You had a good reason. Just like you had a good reason when you let your fucking dealer dump a body behind Declan's bar."

With tears in her eyes, she shook her head. "It wasn't like that."

"Then what was it like, Ria?" I snapped. "What was it like when you were fishing around in my safe for the little bit of money I have stashed away? What was it like when he killed that girl? What the fuck is going on? What did you do?"

Straightening, practically holding her breath to keep from crying, she set the money on my dresser. "It's complicated."

"Then explain it to me, god damn it!" It was without thought when I raised my arms at my sides and all but screamed a laugh. "Explain to me what the hell is going on. Tell me how deep you are so we can fucking fix it. Because right now, Declan is on the line because of what you did. That son of the bitch detective is trying to get him put away for murder, and I don't know how to fix it if I don't know what the fuck is going on, Ria."

"I—I'm going to make this right. I'm not going to let Declan go down for this. I just need a little time, and some money, and—"

"Then fucking take it!" I pointed to the money she'd dropped on the dresser. "Fucking take it, then tell me what's going on." And now that I got a good look at her, noting the dark circles beneath her eyes, her ghastly pallor, I realized, yet again, that she was in withdrawals. "Is this all because you owe a dealer money? They're trying to take me and Declan down because you owe them money? How much? And of all the people you could steal from, why me? Why not a god damned bank? You're a teleporter, Ria. And you're stealing from your family? Instead of the fucking corporations or some shit?"

That one must've stunned her, because all she did was open and shut her mouth a few times. After a moment, she shook her head. "No. Yes, I mean—It's complicated, okay? It's about money. It's about *a lot* of money. But it's more than that. It's about me." The tears in her eyes erupted. A soft weep escaped her dry, crackly lips. Normally, I would've reached out and held her, but I was in no mood. "He's not just my dealer, okay? I... It's bigger than that."

"What's bigger than that?" I asked. "And how much fucking money? Who is this guy? What did you do to him?"

"He thinks I fucked him over," she said, composing herself enough to get the words out. "I didn't. But I guess I kinda did? So did Alicia. He started as my dealer. Then I got behind on money. He fronted me some shit, and I didn't give him enough back, and he knew what I did to make money, so he..." Lifting both hands before her face, her shoulders sunk inward. She muffled her sobs into her palms, whole body trembling. "It was just supposed to be a couple of johns. But he didn't want me working at the club. Not unless he could be there, and my boss didn't like him hanging around, and I almost lost my job. Then he or one of his guys was on my ass all the time. Everywhere I went, everything I did, everything I *do*, they're always there. Me and Alicia, we were trying to get out from under him, and—We were stupid. We were so fucking stupid."

"Wait," I murmured, beginning to tie it together. Gradually, my stomach dropped all the way out of my ass. "Wait, are you telling me that this motherfucker is your pimp, Ria?"

Letting out another sob, she shook her head. "I didn't want him to be. I didn't—This wasn't supposed to happen. It just all got so out of hand. I didn't mean to—"

"Are you fucking kidding me?" Stepping closer, sticking a finger in her face, I spoke through gritted teeth. "When you started doing this, I told you that I understood. But I told you to never get a pimp. You promised me you wouldn't. We talked about how fucking predatory they are, and how they ruin the girls' lives, and how they treat them like property, and—"

"I know!" She grabbed fistfuls of hair as she wept. "I know, okay?! I didn't mean to! It just—It just happened! But he wouldn't stop. He *won't* stop. The same thing happened to Alicia, so we tried to get out however we could. Our clients are here, all of our lives are here, so we couldn't leave, and he has trackers anyway, so we thought if we—" She cut herself off with another sob.

And there it was. Now it all made sense.

We were lucky he hadn't tried to kill us. Instead, he had settled for ruining our lives.

"You tried to kill him. That's why he killed Alicia."

Still sobbing, she nodded. "But I found somebody. He's gonna do it. He's going to get rid of Davey, and everything'll be fine. I just need to give him enough money, and we'll never hear from him again."

"He killed your friend for this shit, and you think that getting involved with somebody who's going to kill him is going to be any fucking better?! Are you out of your god damned mind, Ria? He's going to do the same thing to you as Davey did! You're gonna be in the same situation, just with a different villain. This is all going to start again. You can't be that fucking stupid, can you?"

"Fuck you," she made out between sobs. "Fuck you, Brooke."

"Fuck *me*?" I laughed. "Yeah, fuck me, you ungrateful little bitch. I bend over backwards for you, and you just keep shitting all over me! You fuck up my life all the god damned time, and that's bad enough, but now you're ruining Declan's too, and 'fuck me,' for pointing out how stupid you are for messing with the same fire that got you burned in the first place?!"

"How dare you judge me?!" Didn't know where I judged her there. Just stated facts. Maybe they hurt, but they were the honest to gods truth, and I wouldn't take back a single word that'd come out of my mouth. "You have everything. You don't get it. You don't get what it's like out there. We have to do what we have to do to survive—"

"Out *there*?!" I gestured out the window. "On the streets? The same streets that I grew up on? Oh, no, I'm clueless. I'm just oh-so-sheltered. Dealing with you twenty-four seven, I just have no idea what it's like, right? I'm just so ignorant to this pathetic, street war shit—"

"You are!" She gestured around the room. "Look at how you live. Look how fucking normal you are. You act like it's so tough for you because of how we grew up, but you got out! You have no idea how fucking hard it is to—"

"You could get out too! You could get your fucking shit together, Ria! You could stop blaming the world and look in the fucking mirror. Because this is on you. All of this is your god damned fault. You are why your life looks the way it does. You're shaming me for getting my life together? Or being normal? You act like you didn't have the same fucking opportunities that I did. But in reality, you had more. Because you had me. I had *no one*. I *did* take care of you, and I didn't have someone like that. I didn't have someone that I could look up to, somebody I could go to when I needed help. But you did. You had me. And now I'm the bad guy? Because I just don't get what it's like to be an addict? Try loving one. Try watching someone you love kill themselves every god damned day, and then tell me how hard you have it. Tell me how hard you have it when you're about to lose your relationship, the only thing that has ever made sense to you, the only thing that has ever brought you any joy, because of your junkie fucking sister!"

I shouldn't have said that. The moment it left my lips, I regretted it. It was an awful, horrible, mean thing to say. It was the truth, but I could've said it without the slur. I knew that was wrong, and I would regret it for a very long time. But the damage was already done, I could see it on my little sister's face.

"Sure." Letting out a shocked laugh, she swatted her tears away. "Blame me. *I'm* the reason Declan doesn't want you. I don't know why he ever fucked you in the first place, but you're the reason that he won't stay." She gave me a once over, laughing again. "I mean come on, look at you. Look at him. The guy could have anyone he wants, and he chooses this?" A wave over me in gesture. "When was the last time you ate a salad? Or went for a run? You could at least try to look good for him, if you're not going to tell him you love him, but I guess even that's too much work. You can sit here and pretend like you love him so much, that losing him is destroying you, but you won't do a fucking thing for the guy. I might be a junkie whore, but you couldn't sell it for nickel. I'm surprised Declan doesn't make you pay *him*." Grabbing the money off the dresser, she tore the rubber band off. One by one, she swept the twenties and fifties and hundreds onto the floor. "Keep your money. Go buy yourself some company."

And she disappeared.

I just stood there, staring at the money on the ground. Trying to remember everything that was said, and failing each time. Only remembering those last few bits.

She wasn't wrong. In fact, everything she said was everything I feared the most.

Ria was the pretty one. I was the smart one. That was always how it'd been. I liked being that. The smart, responsible, mature big sister. It didn't matter that I was always the tall, bitchy, fat one because I didn't want the typical, nuclear family, American dream anyway. I wanted a career. I wanted pretty bookshelves and nice floors and a house that smelled like flowers and honey.

I never cared. I told myself I didn't, at least.

Then Declan had entered my life, and for once, I felt like I was more than that. He loved that I was a dorky librarian. All those things that I thought separated me from my femininity, my sexuality, turned him on. He loved my body, my demeanor, and for the first time, I felt adored and desired.

Now I was losing him.

And now I had lost Ria too.

But at least I had my bookshelves. At least my house smelled pretty, even if I didn't.

Tears raining from my eyes, chest so tight it felt like it would implode, I collapsed slowly to the floor. A heaving gasp dropped from my lips, and I screamed. I cried, and I prayed with everything I had that I could flick two days into the past. Maybe, just maybe, if I tried hard enough, I could turn back time and erase all of this. And not feel everything that I was feeling right now. Because there was nothing I wanted more than to feel nothing at all.

Normally, I had no problem doing that. Shutting it off. But this time? It all came down. Every wall inside my mind, around my heart, crumbled into a thousand little pieces.

There was one thing I knew would take the edge off. And, much to my joy, when I teleported to the kitchen, my bottle of vodka still sat on the top. Grabbing it, spinning off the lid, I had no doubt. This would do the trick.

I tilted my head back, and I chugged.

CHAPTER EIGHTEEN

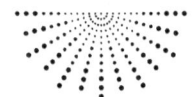

EMORY

All but stomping into the bar, Declan wore the expression of his other form. His brows were furrowed, but his eyes were glassy. Like he was simultaneously pissed and sad all at once.

Emory knew why. He *understood* why. That didn't make it easier. Neither did the fact that he came to the counter and poured another full glass of whiskey.

Emory had to tell him. He didn't want to, but, judging by the fiasco that had just gone down, he had no choice. Declan knew a little bit of everything, and Emory knew just a hair more. He couldn't keep it from his best friend any longer. But, of course, he knew that he had to break it gently.

"You okay?" Emory asked, wiping a glass and returning it to its place on the shelf beneath the bar.

Declan snorted. "Define 'okay.'"

Judging by the second glass that Declan was pouring, he was far from Emory's definition of okay. "With Brooke, I mean. You guys alright?"

"I'm mad at her. More mad at her sister than at her, but I'm mad at them both. But Ria takes the cake." Declan leaned against the bar. "But I shouldn't have gone off on her like that. This isn't much easier for her than it is for me. "

All Emory could manage out was, "I am so sorry, man."

"Not like any of this is your fault." Declan eased out a deep breath. "I just don't know what to do."

"It is though. My fault, I mean." Those words tasted like vinegar coming out of Emory's mouth. The look Declan gave him, the anger that had been directed at Brooke earlier, now fell on him. "Not completely. I didn't actually *do* anything. But I knew that Ria was friends with Alicia. I knew that she was keeping it quiet, and I saw her around back the night of the murder. She was smoking a cigarette when I took the trash out. I knew she ran off, but I wasn't sure if she had anything to do with what happened to Alicia until today."

Slowly, Declan's expression softened. "You didn't tell me because you don't want me to be pissed at her."

"I guess." Biting his lip, Emory nodded. "I just didn't know what was going on. I *still* don't know what's going on. I just didn't want throw her under the bus, you know?"

"Those Lewis girls," Declan muttered, "they've got a way of messing with your head."

Declan had no idea.

"It's alright." The phone on the back wall rang, and Declan started toward it. "We need to talk to her though. We figure out what's going on, we have a hell of a better chance of keeping me out of jail."

That simple.

It was always that simple with Declan. He was irate in a minute, but just as quick to cool down. Even though he was upset, even though he had every right to be, he cared about Ria. Underneath that rough exterior, Declan was a big softy. Hence the blowout with Brooke.

Emory felt bad for that too.

He didn't hear exactly what Declan had been saying, only caught "detective," and some mumbled curses. Rubbing his eyes together, rubbing his eyes between his thumb and forefinger, breathing slow to maintain his composure, Emory's heart broke a little more

He shouldn't have told him about his and Ria's bet. All it'd done was pour fuel on the flames. Why add more stress at a time like this? It had been intended as a playful joke when he had brought it up, but now it was too heavy. The guy was going through enough, and he didn't need any more shit on his plate.

But that was exactly what Emory had done to him. Tensions were already high in his relationship because Ria was partially to blame for this, if not *entirely* the to blame for this, and Emory just had to go and make it worse.

While Emory may have seemed like an asshole to everyone who met him, there was a heart in there. Was it black as tar? Probably. But he had never intended to harm anyone. Especially not his best friend.

Declan was crazy about Brooke, and Emory wanted to believe the Brooke felt the same way. Even if she was horrible at showing it. But he shouldn't have meddled. He shouldn't have run his mouth. Especially because, at the end of the day, even if Brooke wasn't perfect, until the past few nights, she was close enough to perfect for Declan.

Returning the phone to the receiver, Declan let out another one of those deep, trembling sighs. "Guess I gotta go back down to the station. They want my fingerprints now. Got a warrant and everything."

"Why?" Emory's heart pumped faster. "Did they find something?"

"I guess the girl was wearing something. A belt or some shit, I don't know. They found fingerprints, and they want to check mine. It was the final cause of death, apparently. They thought it was blunt force trauma, but it was strangulation with an object. So as long as my prints aren't on that belt, I should be free and clear," Declan said. "I hope. God, I fucking hope."

"I'll call your lawyer. Let her know where you're headed. Just don't say a word."

"I know the routine," Declan said under his breath. "Just keep an eye on things here, would you?"

As always, Emory promised he would, then watched with a heavy heart as Declan walked out the door. Emory called the lawyer. The bar patrons would have to wait until this business was attended to. After all, if Declan ended up in prison, this place wouldn't exist anymore.

Just as he hung up the phone, a familiar voice said, "Just put it on my tab," directly behind him.

When he spun around, Brooke was reaching beneath the bar, grabbing a bottle of vodka. That was her drink of choice. Vodka cranberry. This time, though, she was ditching the cranberry. The bottle went straight to her lips.

"It's been a shit day, right?" Emory asked. "Do you want to make it worse with your head bent over the toilet?"

"Hey, well, at least I won't feel it." Tilting her head back, Brooke chugged.

Brooke barely drank. A vodka cranberry once or twice a week. On a special occasion, more than that, but Emory had never seen her take a shot. He certainly hadn't seen her drink straight from the bottle.

But, all things considered, could he blame her?

"Can you sit, at least?" Emory asked. "Don't need you falling and breaking your neck. Especially while Declan's at the police station."

Brooke's head whipped around to face him, her face flushed. She had clearly already had a few. "What? Is he okay? What happened?"

"From what I could tell, he's fine," he said, guiding Brooke around the bar and on to a stool. He made sure this one had a back. It was times like this he wished they made highchairs for adults. "Just fingerprints. Should be a good thing, really. It could prove he wasn't the killer."

"Jesus Christ," Brooke said. "And it's all because of Ria. Because Ria had to be a god damned idiot and get a fucking pimp."

Slowly, Emory's brows furrowed. "What?"

"Yep." Like a baby with a bottle, Brooke tilted her head back and chugged some more. One of those grown-up highchairs would be great right about now. Maybe Emory should've patented that idea. "Tried to kill the guy. That's what all of this is about. That's why he killed Alicia, that's why he tried to frame Declan, or at least make his life miserable. That's why he broke into my house. Just to fuck with us and punish her."

"That's crazy." Emory was past confused. More than once, Emory and Ria had discussed her work, and she'd always sworn that she worked alone. With a few other girls from time to time, but never a pimp. Pimps were a giant chunk of what made sex work so dangerous. Emory said so, ending with, "Ria knows how stupid that is."

"Yeah, she does," Brooke muttered, propping her elbows on the counter to keep her head upright. "Now she's trying to get another one to get rid of the first one. And *I'm* the bad guy. Somehow, I'm the fucking bad guy for telling her how fucking stupid that is. You should tell her." Brooke wagged a finger at him. "She listens to you. You should be the one to tell her how stupid she's been. Because otherwise, the dumb bitch is gonna end up dead. She's gonna fucking kill herself. Or get herself killed. One or the other." Brooke's words slurred. "And somehow, that'll be my fault. No, it *is*.

"It *is* my fault. The way she turned out, the drugs, everything, it's all my fault. I did this. I created this monster. I should've done better. I shouldn't have worked for the Chambers. I should've just taken care of Ria. But *nooo*. I had to get a degree and break the cycle.

"And what's it matter? What difference does it make if I broke it? I probably won't have kids, and it'll genuinely shock me if she doesn't have any. Eventually, she'll get pregnant, if she hasn't been already, and then what? Am I supposed to raise the kid when she dies? Because that's what's gonna happen." Tears filling her eyes, she met Emory's gaze. Brooke shook her head so hard, he worried it would fall off her shoulders. "She's gonna die. This life is going to fucking kill her. I'm going to bury my baby sister, and I don't know how to handle that. I don't know what I'm supposed to do. How am I supposed to help her? How do I fix it, Emory? What do I do?"

A lump formed in his throat.

Emory had known things were bad, but he didn't know it was *this* bad.

He didn't want to think about that possibility any more than Brooke did, but he wasn't stupid. That's where Ria was headed. That was the way the life worked. You died. You got in too deep, and you wound up dead.

Aside from that, while they couldn't stand each other most of the time, Emory cared about Brooke. Not just because Declan did, but because when you're around somebody so much, you see the good in them. Brooke was a bitch. There was no denying that. But like Emory, there was good in that black, tarry heart.

And, after all, they had something in common. Their love for Ria. Emory's was different than Brooke's, of course, but at the end of the day, love was love. And while they didn't share much, they shared that.

"You were a kid," Emory said. "Where Ria is, the life she's living now, that's not on you. She's the only one who can change it."

"I could kill the guy for her," Brooke said. "That way, she doesn't have to work with this other piece of shit. That wouldn't be a bad idea, right?"

No, it sure as shit would be. "The cops are breathing down our necks. We can't kill anyone."

Breathing out slowly, Brooke took another gulp from the bottle. "I know. But I really want to kill somebody right now. And better the pimp than my sister. But I could. I could take her out myself."

Emory fought the laugh that built in his chest. There was no stopping the smile though. "Brooke, I know you're upset about what this is doing to Declan, but we're going to get through it. It's gonna be fine. Whatever Ria did, we'll fix it. As soon as we've cleared Declan's name, we'll fix it."

"That's not what I'm mad about." Again, Brooke lifted the bottle and took a swig. "I'm mad because she's mean. She was right, but she's fucking mean."

Leaning against the bar behind him, Emory frowned. "What'd she do?"

Now, instead of Declan, it was Brooke who eased out a deep breath. "Just told the truth, I guess. She wasn't wrong. None of it was wrong. Just mean."

Emory's frown deepened. While he had never been on the receiving end of Ria's mouth, he'd seen her dish out plenty. "What did she say, Brooke?"

"I called her a junkie." Brooke hung her head between her shoulders. "That wasn't nice. I shouldn't have done that. It's a sensitive topic, you know? I should've handled it better. I should've done better. I should know better with her."

That much had been established. "What did she say, Brooke?"

"That if I lose Declan, it's my fault." She couldn't meet his gaze anymore. Her eyes were stuck to the tabletop. "That I'm fat. Ugly, too, I think. Implied it, at least. That she doesn't know why Declan ever fucked me to begin with. And, I mean, neither do I." She laughed, but there was no humor in it. "Said that I don't deserve him. He's gonna leave me one day. She's surprised he's lasted as long as he has. And, I mean, she's right."

Looking up again, tears staining her cheeks, she sniffled. "I'm ruining it. I'm fucking it up. He deserves better than me. He deserves somebody who's put together, and good, and not me. And prettier. I mean, have you looked at that man? He's... And I'm..." She gestured over herself. "It's the bond. That's the only reason he stays. I'm not enough for him, and we all know it. Everybody who looks at us together knows it."

Emory's frown deepened. "That's not true, Brooke."

And it wasn't. She was full of shit if she thought that Declan was out of her league. Was Brooke on the heavier side? Yeah. And that was one among many things that Declan loved about her. She had a stomach, thick thighs, and massive hips that he adored. That he often told Emory how much he adored, despite Emory's lack of care for the subject.

The emotional unavailability, that was a problem. But her appearance? That was just a low blow Ria threw because Brooke tossed one out first.

"Yeah, it is," Brooke slurred, dropping her head to the counter. "I'm not good enough for him. I can't even tell him how much he means to me. He's going to get sick of me. And he'll leave. He'll leave just like everybody leaves."

If only she were being this vulnerable with Declan instead of Emory.

Not a huge fan of emotional professions himself, Emory summoned up the willpower to walk around the bar and sit beside her. He put his hand on her back and patted a few times. It probably looked like a mother trying to burp a child, but he did his best. "He's crazy about you, Brooke. And I promise, your body is not a problem for him."

Peering up at him, face smashed by her hand from the awkward angle, she said, "Really?"

"Really. Declan's never been into small girls." Another awkward pat on her back. "He likes a challenge. He's a big dude. Small girl wouldn't put up enough of a fight for him."

Brooke laughed, then hiccupped. Her face screwed up in disgust. "Gross. Baby barf."

Emory was sure she would be having some full-blow, adult barfs later. "You gotta open up to him though. I know you had to do a lot of things you wish you hadn't to survive. I get it." Given the way Emory was raised, the homophobic parents who had abandoned him, Emory understood. At least to some degree. "We've all got trauma. It's going to interact with our relationships. But that's our responsibility. It's not theirs. The only way to make this better, the only way to make your relationship with him stronger is if you open up, Brooke."

"It's... It's hard." Brooke murmured, eyes falling shut.

"It is. But you've done a lot harder."

All Brooke said was, "Mm."

Grunting his annoyance, Emory shook her shoulder. "Come on. Let me help you back to Declan's place."

"Uh-uh," Brooke said.

"Fine. The office then."

Brooke waved him off. "Too far."

"Well, you can't just sleep on the counter."

"Yes, I can!" she yelled, her eyes still shut.

Someone in the back of the bar yelled, "Yeah, she can!" A chorus of laughter followed.

Rolling his eyes, Emory stood. Hopefully, Declan would be back soon. She'd be his problem then. For now, Emory would just make sure nobody tried to stuff her in the back of their car.

CHAPTER NINETEEN

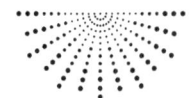

DECLAN

Getting fingerprinted was no big thing.

I knew to keep my mouth shut, so, that was what I did. I didn't discuss the case with any of the officers who spoke with me, didn't say a word that could get me in trouble. Just my name, and my birthday. Apparently, they needed that. They also required I show them my driver's license, but no words were required for that.

Still, it was close to an hour before I was out of there. Along the way home, I texted Brooke and asked her to call me. She didn't respond. Not unusual.

It wasn't that she blew me off when she was mad. She just needed space. Too much of it, though, for my liking.

I loved her. Even if she wouldn't tell me she loved me, I loved her more than anything. So, I tolerated it. But I meant what I said earlier. A time was gonna come when I'd run out of patience. I'd gotten close to it today.

But that wasn't her fault. Everything that was going on with Ria, I knew it wasn't Brooke's fault. Brooke didn't choose the life she was born into. Things were worse for her than they were for most.

Brooke had a lot of issues, and she needed to work on them. I couldn't make her do that, though. That was something she needed to do on her own. Whether or not she would was what would decide what came next for us.

Yet, the moment that thought ran through my mind, I felt the worst sinking sensation in my gut. Losing her terrified me. It was hard to believe given the way that I had acted this afternoon, but that was the truth. Neither of us were great with emotions. But she was virtually emotionless most of the time, and I just wanted to see her feel something. *Anything.*

Not this, though. Not what I saw when I walked into the bar.

Flapping his lips together in a trill, Emory looked between me and Brooke. Who was draped over the countertop. In her palm, she fisted a bottle of vodka. Her forearm, however, she used as a pillow. Even from here, I could smell the booze mixed with her perfume.

"Jesus Christ," I said under my breath, walking that way. "How much did she drink?"

"Too much, clearly," Emory said

"Clearly." Setting a hand on her back, I coasted it up and down slowly. "Brooke."

All I got was a vague moan in response. Not the kind I liked, either.

"Sweetheart, wake up." Gently, I shook her shoulder. She barely flinched. "Let's get you to bed."

Eyes fluttering open, she made what she could of a smile. "Declan."

"That was my name, last I checked." I tucked some hair behind her ear. "How you feeling?"

Smile dissipating, she shook her head. "Not good."

"With your breath smelling like that, I can't say I'm surprised. Can you walk?"

She nodded, then took the hand I offered her. The moment her feet touched the ground, her upper half attempted to do the same. I caught her before she fell, then shot Emory a look over the bar. "What the hell happened?"

"Ria, I'm assuming,"

"What, did Ria open her mouth and pour the bottle down it?" Bearing almost all of Brooke's weight, barely able to keep her on two feet, I glared at him. "Wasn't it you pouring her shots?"

"Hey, she's your girl," Emory said, crossing his arms against his chest. "She didn't exactly ask for permission when she came behind the bar and grabbed the bottle."

Of course she didn't. Did Brooke ever ask for permission for anything?

"I'm sorry," she slurred. "I'll pay for it."

As if I was worried about the money. "Let's just get you back to my house. Get some water in you. And maybe some sleep."

She slurred another apology, and I only kissed her forehead in response. This was far from the way that I had envisioned her being vulnerable with me, but it was kind of nice. Practically carrying her back to my house was a small feat. But at least for once, she needed me. It wasn't how I would've liked for her to have needed me, but it was something.

We had only just crossed the threshold when she muttered, "I don't feel good."

I could already hear her stomach gurgling, so I hurriedly grabbed the trashcan by the entryway and held it out beneath her. Somehow, managing to do so without her vomiting all over me. Had to give her credit, her aim was good. Granted, there was puke through her hair now, but she didn't make a mess on my floor, and I was grateful for that.

I helped her onto a chair, holding the trash bin the whole time. Between dry heaves, she apologized again and again. With each one, I told her it was okay. Maybe it should've been me with my head in the trashcan, given the fact that I was the one being accused of murder, but I got it. It wasn't her fault, but she thought it was.

"I know what Ria did has nothing to do with you," I said, tucking some hair behind her ear. Ignored the vomit that got on my fingers. "It's alright. Let's just get you feeling better, okay?"

Resting her head in my hand, letting me cradle her face, she shook her head. "Not that. That too, I guess, but not that."

"Then what are you apologizing for, sweetheart?"

"Sucking at this." Her voice was hardly audible. But there was no denying it now. There were tears in her eyes. "I don't know what a healthy relationship looks like. I don't know how to be in one. I don't know how to be a good partner. I don't know how to show you how much you matter. Because you do. You and Ria, you're all that matter to me. I'm sorry I'm such a bitch, and I'm sorry I don't know how to love you. Not the right way. But I do. I do love you."

A fire kindled in my chest. Warm and cozy, like cuddling up beside one on a winter night after trekking through the snow all day.

But before I could say anything, before I could tell her how much I appreciated hearing that, she was rambling again.

"That doesn't mean anything. The words don't mean anything. The last thing my mom said when she left was 'I love you.' Then she walked out, and I never saw her again." Those tears dropped over in a waterfall. "So I don't say it, because it doesn't mean anything. Being there, being with you, sitting on the couch together, reading books, watching TV, those kinds of things. That matters. The words don't mean anything. And I'm a librarian." I couldn't tell if she laughed or sobbed when she said that last bit. "I love words. But they're pretend. They're another universe. Another world. But they aren't real."

Lifting her fingers into my hair, reaching around the back of my neck, she tried to smile. It didn't stop the tears, though. "This is real. I'm ruining it, but it's real. I don't how to fix it. I know I'm breaking it, but I don't want to. I don't want to lose you. I don't want you to leave, too. I want this to work. I don't want to fight to make it work. I just want it to work, and I know it's my fault. I know I'm why it doesn't work. I know I'm fucking it up, but I just—"

A lurch cut her off. She bent over into the trashcan and hurled again, growling like a dinosaur into the bin.

While she puked, everything shifted. The world around me first, and then my entire perspective on this relationship.

It all made sense. Everything made sense now.

Before I fell for her, I knew what I was getting into. So how could I be surprised by any of this?

Shit, it hurt. I was hurt because I knew that she was hurting. And I knew that I hadn't been helping.

Getting through Brooke's walls required a bulldozer. Or, that was what I had thought, at least. But maybe half the issue here was me. Maybe instead of fighting with her all the time, maybe instead of making her feel like shit, making her terrified she would lose me, I needed a ladder. Rather than breaking through and shattering those walls apart, maybe I needed to climb over them. Maybe I needed to sit on the ledge for a while and look at her from the outside. Maybe I didn't need to dive into the center of her heart right away. Maybe I needed to observe. Understand.

That memory, the one of her mom walking out, saying that she loved her as she did, was a piece of something I needed to see.

Granted, it wasn't my fault she had failed to share that with me. But it wasn't her obligation either. I was more open than she was, there was no denying that, but why did I feel entitled to her life story? That wasn't my right.

This was. Holding her hair back as she puked. That was my right as the man who loved her. But forcing her to fall apart, to crumble, when I could just sit on the edge and observe was the safer way for both of us.

While she puked, I murmured a, "shh," sound. I whispered that it was okay. And when she finally stopped, I lifted her chin to meet my gaze. She was still crying, and I wiped her tears away. "I'm not going anywhere."

"Everyone says that," she whispered. "But words don't matter. Words aren't real."

"But this is." Giving a smile, I cupped her cheek in my hand. "You don't have to believe me. I know it's gonna take a long time before you believe me. But you're my world, Brooke. I'm here, and I'm not going anywhere."

"Unless my sister gets you sent to jail." Letting out another soft sob, which teetered on laughter, she shook her head. "She's horrible. I love her, but she's fucking horrible. I'm so sorry. I'm so sorry she brought all this to you. You don't deserve this."

"You don't deserve what she puts you through either." Normally, I wouldn't say something like that. Ria was more than her little sister. She was practically Brooke's kid. She bent over backwards every day to take care of her. I respected that, I loved her for that, but clearly, it was killing her. Doing everything that she did for Ria was killing Brooke. "What'd she do? Emory said she was why you got so drunk."

"It's her pimp. That's why this all happened. They tried to kill him, and he killed Alicia, and now Ria is in the middle of it. To hurt her, they decided to fuck with her family. And I told her how stupid this was." Lips curling, the tears came down in a storm again.

"I told her she's ruining her life, and she's an idiot, and she needs to get her shit together, because I don't want to fucking bury her. I don't want her to die. But she won't listen. She just *won't fucking listen*, and I know I'll lose her, and she was right. Everything she said, she was right. I don't know why you stick around either. I don't know why you put up with me and all this shit. You could have anyone, and you choose me. And eventually, you're gonna get sick of it. Just like I'm getting sick of her. And I don't want to lose her, and I don't want to lose you, but I don't—I don't—I don't know what to do." She was sobbing by the time she made it to that last sentence.

There was no relief this time. As much as I had wanted to see her vulnerable, as much as I appreciated that she was giving me that for the first time, this wasn't what I wanted. Not for her to her feel like this. So broken. So torn.

I would never make her choose between Ria and me. But Ria did need to keep my name out of her mouth. Not only because my relationship with her sister was none of her damn business, but because she was wrong. And it was cruel.

I didn't care what was said that led Ria to manipulate her that way, because it wasn't relevant. Brooke did everything for that girl, and she spit in her face every time. She loved her, I knew she loved her, but she used the hell out of her.

Brooke was a resource to Ria. Ria was family, friendship, and sisterhood, to Brooke. And Ria capitalized on that, and it pissed me off every time. For the most part, I kept my nose out of their relationship, but not this time.

Taking Brooke's face in my hands again, wiping the various liquids from her face, I said, "She was wrong." A breath that almost resembled a whimper left Brooke's lips. "I don't know what she said, but if she used me to hurt you, she was wrong. I'm not going anywhere."

A sniffle, and a nod. I still wasn't sure she believed it, but she heard it.

"I know you just want to help her. I know she means the world to you. But she's an adult now, Brooke. She's not your responsibility anymore. If she chooses to live this way, you can't stop her."

"But what if she dies?" she whispered through trembling lips. "What if this life kills her? How am I supposed to live with that?"

"The same way me and my mom do." Thumbing her cheek, I frowned. "You just keep going. You did what you could, sweetheart. But it's your choice if you let her keep hurting you."

Her lips quivered, and she sniffled again. But she nodded. "I know."

Blowing out a slow, careful breath, I looked her over. Between the puke in her hands and hair, all over her shirt, there was no cleaning this up with some paper towels. "How about we get you a shower and into bed?"

Grasping hold of the entry table, she started to stand. The table trembled, and everything on top of it did the same.

I gripped it in place before it could fall. "How about you let me help you?"

I half expected her to tell me to fuck off. To say that she was a grown woman, she didn't need help in the shower. But she set the puke bin on the floor and reached out for my hand.

CHAPTER TWENTY

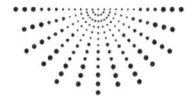

DECLAN

When Mom's lupus got bad, we got her a shower chair. It was a slow progression, but the fatigue came on early. She couldn't stand for long periods of time.

I never got rid of that shower chair after she had moved to an assisted living facility. So, when Brooke couldn't stand on her own, that was how I helped her bathe. She sat, and I wiped her off, and washed her hair, and made her drink Gatorade while I did.

She kept apologizing. She didn't need to.

It wasn't that I wanted a girlfriend who needed my help with everything. I didn't need to be her parent. But for once, Brooke was struggling, and I got to help her. I got to feel like she needed me. I doubted I would get that opportunity often, but tonight, I had it. And I enjoyed it. In my own twisted, warped perception of love, I enjoyed being needed.

By eleven, I had her tucked into bed. I didn't get much sleep. I kept waking up to hold her hair back while she puked. But, by three, her phone was ringing. I ignored it. She was too out of it to hear it. But then it rang again, and again, and again. As soon as it would go to voicemail, it would ring once more.

Eventually, I stood, wobbled across the house in my disoriented haze, and dug for it in her purse. Couldn't say I was surprised at the name that flashed across the screen. Ria.

I was in no state to talk to her. Not really. Whatever she had said, whatever had happened, had hurt Brooke. And Ria hurt her all the time, even if tonight was the first time she had opened up about it. I resented Ria for that.

But I loved the little shit. She wasn't my sister, but she was close enough to one now. So, I answered. "Brooke's passed out. What's going on, Ria?"

"C-can you wake her up?" Her voice quivered, and a sniffle followed. "I-I need my sister."

"No, she's not waking up anytime soon. Whatever happened between the two of you did a number on her. What's going on, Ria?"

"Just wake her up—"

"No." My tone was firm. I couldn't make Brooke stop enabling her, but right now, she wasn't capable of doing whatever it was Ria needed. For once, Brooke was the one who needed a safe place, and she was in it. She didn't need to deal with Ria's shit right now. But I could. "Do you need help? Or a ride or some shit?"

A breathy sound, almost impossible to identify. A snort? A laugh? A sob? I didn't know. "I need Brooke."

"Well, you broke Brooke's heart tonight. She drank half my bar, and she's passed out in my bed." I didn't mean to sound like a dick, but those were the facts. "What's going on? Can I help?"

A moment of silence, and another one of those odd sounds. Then a cry, I was certain of this time. "I-I'll figure it—"

"No, you won't figure it out. I'll come help you." Wasn't sure if I sounded more like a big brother or a controlling father there, but the fact remained. She sounded bad, and I wasn't going to leave her to walk home in the dark from gods knew where. "Where are you? What happened?"

"I—it—" Some more sniffling, and the rustling of wind. "I can just walk. I'll—"

"God damn it, Ria," I snapped, grabbing my keys off the wall. 'Course, I'd have to run to Brooke's and grab her car, because even if Ria was stable enough to hold herself up on the back of my bike, that seat was reserved for Brooke. "Right now. Tell me where you..." I stopped. Blinking hard, the keys jingled as I dropped my hand to my side. "Wait. Why can't you teleport?"

Another difficult to describe, breathy sound. "I don't want to talk to about this, Declan."

"Fine. Don't talk to me about it. But I'm coming to get you from wherever the hell you are, and you're gonna explain it to Brooke in the morning. Alright?"

"She probably doesn't want to talk to me anyway," she murmured, her voice almost undetectable. "I'll just—I can—"

"You'll just tell me where the fuck you are, and I'll come and bring you back here."

A long moment of silence. Eventually, she broke it with, "You know the place. You helped Brooke trash it this afternoon."

I broke a thousand laws on my way there. Amazingly, I didn't get pulled over. Good thing, too, all things considered.

I wished I could say I was even the slightest bit surprised when I finally found Ria. She was seated on the main road that bordered the long driveway to Davey's home. Practically curled in a ball, Ria stared at the ground. When I pulled up beside her, she didn't even raise her gaze to look at me. The side of her head rested against a tree.

When I called for her out the window, she didn't respond. Didn't even budge. And for a moment, I feared that Brooke was right. That now would be the time that she buried her little sister.

Practically sprinting from the car, I left the door open. I called her name several times, none of which she answered to. I dropped to my knees beside her, shaking her shoulder, and her eyes finally opened.

Or at least, as much as they could through the swelling.

Describing her as beaten felt like an understatement.

This... The way she looked, it was near death. I barely recognized her. If not for the smell, the smell of her blood, I probably wouldn't have. Another scent wafted from her that tainted her own. A smell that I knew well and had no desire to smell from my girlfriend's little sister. I'd smelled it on Brooke this afternoon though, right before she teleported home. The smell of sex. Which I smelled often enough on Ria, but it was different this time. Tainted with blood.

Both eyes nearly swollen shut, lips busted and purple, four times their usual thickness, she struggled out, "You didn't have to come."

And now, I understood.

Now I understood why Brooke bent over backwards for this little shit. Despite her faults, no matter how many of them, she looked so innocent. So fragile.

She was. That's how she ended up in these situations. She fucked up, and she got fucked over, a thousand times. Who else would be there for her? If not Brooke, if not me, who would be here right now? Another pimp? One who would do the exact same, if not worse, to her?

"Davey? Is that who did this?" I glanced down the driveway. "How many of them are up there? Just him? Or—"

"Just take me home." Lips quivering, she pulled in a deep breath to retain her composure. "Please. *Please,* just take me home."

I didn't want to. I wanted to do the very thing that started this mess. Kill the motherfucker who thought it was okay to treat women like this. To treat *anyone* like this. To take advantage of the people who were struggling and use them as tools for personal gain. For money, for drugs, for whatever it was that kept him in this business.

But it wasn't my place. Coming here, helping Ria, that was to help Brooke. I wouldn't regret that. Making the situation worse? Being the reason this happened to her again? Or the reason something even worse happened?

I wouldn't be able to live with myself. So, with a grunt of annoyance, I held her upper arm tighter. "Can you walk?"

"Probably not." Ria's voice was riddled with shame. "But I can try."

Clenching my teeth, I shook my head. Without giving her another option, I hoisted her into my arms. Certainly felt like a big brother then. Especially because, as I walked back to the car, her head collapsed to the side. Looking down at her was like looking down at an orphaned child. Supposed that was what she was.

When that big brother instinct kicked in, all I could think was, *Get out of this life before it kills you, you dumb little shit.*

As I got her into the back seat, lying with her head propped against the window, the overhead light shone on her thighs. Never paid much attention to anyone's thighs aside from Brooke's, especially not her little sister's, but I was already in *notice any and everything* mode in case I had to rush her to the hospital. And it was hard to miss.

Her fishnets were torn. Not a spot or tow, but just a few inches above her knees all the way up to her... Well, I stopped looking north before I could confirm any more than that.

I wouldn't dare ask, but I had a theory about that scent of blood mixed with sex now.

She was too out of it to realize that I had noticed. Too out of it to adjust her clothes so I couldn't see any more of it. But the fire that lit inside me was unlike anything I had ever felt. So much of me wanted to sprint back into that house and burn it to the ground. Maybe rip Davey's throat out along the way. With my bare hands, with my teeth, I didn't care.

And I didn't care what she had done. Sure, she tried to kill the guy. Probably because this wasn't the first time he had fucking done this to her, and he deserved it. He deserved to be ripped apart like a piece of meat because that was how he saw the people who paid his bills. Meat. Items for him to capitalize on, to get pleasure from, and I had never been more disgusted in my life.

But that wasn't my place. It wasn't my fucking place.

So I just got the blanket Brooke kept in the backseat off the floor and draped it over Ria's body. Then I got in the driver's seat, and I drove home.

Ria was still out of it when we got to the house. Throughout the drive, I turned around to check on her more times than I could count. Each time, she was alive. Barely, but alive.

Emory had been closing up the bar when I'd left. I hadn't spoken to him, just rushed into the car and peeled out of the driveway. It was almost 5 AM though, so he should have been well on his way by now. Instead, he was sitting on my porch.

Once I shifted the car in park and stepped outside, he stood as well. "Where'd you go?"

I only huffed in response. Opening the back door, I said, "Come on, Ria. We're here."

Her eyes fluttered, but she stumbled back when she tried to sit forward. I had to reach inside and cup both hands below her armpits to help her out of the backseat. By the time she was on her feet, Emory was at my side.

"Holy shit," he said, bearing the other half of her weight. "Are you okay, Ari?"

She did the most she could to muster a smile and murmured, "Emory."

He shot me a look that was half heartache, half fury.

"Let's get her inside. I'll tell you what I know once she's settled in."

He accepted that as answer enough, then did for her what I had done for Brooke. He didn't give her a shower, but he did his best to wipe up her blood. Combed the dried-on muck from her hair and away from her face. Helped her into a pair of sweatpants and a sweater that I had lying around. I didn't count on getting those back.

The two of us got her into bed beside Brooke, and then I dropped onto the couch. I'd barely gotten a breath in before Emory snapped, "What the hell happened?"

"I don't know." And that was the truth. I didn't know much of anything for sure. "That guy. The same guy who killed Alicia. He did it. Think he did more than just beat her, too."

Emory's forehead crunched up in confusion.

"I think he... Fuck, I don't know. I don't know, man. It was bad. It was really bad, and she wouldn't let me go back to see what had happened. I didn't get to confront the son of a bitch. I just got her in the car and brought her here. That was what she wanted, so that was what I did."

"What the fuck else could they have done?" Emory asked, still confused and furious. "What does that even mean, Declan?"

Rubbing my eyes between my thumb and forefinger, I shook my head. "There's a smell coming off her, alright? It's a distinct one. But I wasn't sure what it really meant until... Jesus, I shouldn't be telling you this."

"Tell me or I'm gonna go wake her up and make her tell me," he snapped.

"I really don't think she needs a man to *make* her do anything right now, dude." I said firmly. It took a moment, but slowly his eyes widened, and he understood. Bile burned up my throat, and I shook my head again. Like if I shook it enough, I could shake the mental image of it away. "It was bad. That's all I know. Whatever happened to her, it was *really* bad."

"This prick beat and raped her?" Emory's eyes were daggers. "Is that what you're telling me?"

I fought the shudder that coursed down my spine. "I don't know."

"But you think so."

I didn't respond to that. It wasn't my place.

Not another word from him either. He just walked back to my bedroom, where the two of them were sleeping, said something I couldn't hear over the hum of the fan, then walked back through the living room. "I'll be back."

And he disappeared.

I had just dozed off. Brooke and Ria needed the bed more than I did, so I gave it to them. My couch was hard as a rock. I desperately needed a new one, but I doubted I'd be able to afford one anytime soon with the mounting lawyer bills.

But my muscles had just relaxed when a knock sounded at the door. No, *knock* wasn't the word. It was one of those *bam—bam—bam* sounds. Like a cop pounding on a door to raid for drugs. I was half convinced that was the case here until I stood, and that *bam—bam—bam* sounded again. Only then did I realize it was coming from the back door.

The door that couldn't be seen from the road.

Half-asleep, groggy, I stumbled that way. When I opened the door, however, I was wide awake.

And all I could say was, "Shit."

Emory stood on the other side. Blood splattered the entirety of his face, his chest. His hands were swollen, knuckles bloody. Looked like he'd taken a punch or two, judging by the busted lip and the slice on his forehead a quarter of an inch long. "We have a problem."

"No shit, fuckhead." I gestured over him. "That's where you went? You thought you could solve this problem for her. So you fought her pimp. Jesus Christ, how much worse is this gonna get? Is he gonna show here looking for her? Or are you gonna get framed for murder next?"

Scratching his head, Emory pressed his lips together. "No, probably not. But what do you know about covering one up?"

CHAPTER TWENTY-ONE

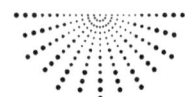

BROOKE

The world was still spinning when I woke up. My stomach didn't hurt so bad, probably because there was nothing left in it.

Not my proudest moment. Eyes fluttering open, I prayed my mistake wouldn't lead me to anything too shameful long term.

Although I didn't remember winding up in Declan's bed, the intricate painting of a wolf in a snow covered forest that hung on the wall told me that was exactly where I was. Which was better than a stranger's bed. So, I couldn't complain. Apparently, I hadn't said anything that had sent him running. A good sign, in my book. Except, when I rolled over, expecting to see his face—

I jolted backward, taking far too long to realize who I was looking at.

Ria. Ria with two black eyes, a busted lip, a cut on her cheek, another on her forehead, and several lining her jaw. And yet, she smiled at me.

"Morning, sissy."

Jaw falling open, I reached out to touch her. As if to tether myself to reality, to confirm that I wasn't dreaming.

She winced when my finger made contact with a bruise on her cheek, but she still managed to smile. "It looks worse than it is."

I highly fucking doubted that. "What happened?"

Wetting her lips, she raised a shoulder. "It doesn't matter."

I sat forward. "Like hell it doesn't matter. What the fuck happened? Was it that asshole who said he'd take care of Davey for you? It was, wasn't it? I knew it. I knew this was just gonna make things worse for you. God damn it. Fuck. Did you walk here? Did—"

"Declan picked me up." Finding my fingers, she twined them between hers. "It doesn't matter right now. None of that shit matters. I'm so, *so* sorry—"

"Who was it?" Straightening, I looked down to check to see if I needed clothes. Thankfully, I was wearing Declan's. Which was good. They were quite comfy, and comfy was good when I needed to fight somebody. And that was exactly what I planned to do. Whoever did this to my little sister was not going to live long enough to fucking regret it. "You tell me right now, or I'm going to Davey's. And I'm going to—"

"Brooke, please." Carefully, she pulled me back to the bed. "I know you're upset. I'm not happy either. But it doesn't matter. I'm leaving."

Breath stopping in my chest, I squinted over her a moment longer. "What do you mean 'you're leaving?'"

"I mean, I'm done." A swallow bobbed her throat. "Last night was bad. It was really bad. And this was it. He let me go. He said he didn't want anything to do with me anymore. No business, no drugs, no nothing. You were right about that other guy. It'd turn out the same way. That's how this life works. That's the cycle. And you broke it." Another smile, almost impossible to decipher beneath all that swelling. "You broke the cycle we were born into, and I'm gonna break it too. I don't want to end up dead. I don't want to end up in debt to somebody like that again.

"I'm gonna get clean. And I'll pay you back every cent you've ever given me. Once I get my shit together, anyway, but I'm just so sorry. I'm so sorry about everything I said yesterday. I was just mad." Tears gathered in her eyes, beading down the edges and onto her cheeks. "That wasn't fair. That was mean. I was a cunt to you for no reason. You have every right to be mad. I'm ruining my life. I'm ruining yours, ruining Declan's, and neither of you deserve this. *I* don't deserve this.

"And I don't want to end up here again. I don't want to fight with you like that again. I don't wanna hurt you, and I don't want you to hurt me, and I just want to fix it. I'm *going* to fix it. Turn my life around, I mean. Maybe I'll go to college, like you did. I don't know. But I know that getting high isn't helping anyone. It's making me miserable, it's making you miserable, and... And could you help me call rehabs today?"

That was the first time she had asked that.

She had never gone to rehab on her own accord. Once, when she was a minor, she'd been forced into one. She got into trouble with the law, and instead of putting her in jail, they sent her to rehab. It didn't do the job then. But she didn't want it done. She had nothing to look forward to. She had no hope. Getting sober was the last thing she wanted.

Probably because it was so bad for us growing up, it felt like it would never end. And when she was in that rehab, I was still in college. Life was just as bad in a different way. I was no longer surrounded by addiction and violence, not outside of Ria, but I was struggling to make ends meet, struggling to make it through the day.

What did she have to look forward to? What role models did she have then? Me? The life I had then? It was hard work with no relief.

And now...

Now, I had a life worth aspiring to. It wasn't perfect, especially considering the whole boyfriend with pending murder charges situation going on, but it wasn't all that bad either. I went to work, I went home, I had great sex with a man I loved, played card games with my friends, and did it all over again.

Maybe this was what she needed. Maybe she needed a rock-bottom and a pretty image to aspire to.

"Yeah, sissy." I managed a smile in response. "We'll call rehabs."

A wider smile, and a nod. Then she sniffled. "I really am sorry. It wasn't true. None of it was true. I was just hurt, and angry, and—"

"It's okay." I squeezed her hand tighter. "It's okay."

And before I could stop her, she was tossing her arms around me, embracing me like I was a tree, and she was a monkey. It was storming, and the branches were swaying, but as long as she held onto me, she believed that. That everything would be okay.

I relished in it for a moment.

Our lives were fucked. This whole situation was a disaster, and I had no idea how to help Declan. But I knew that she was okay. She was miserable, and in a lot of pain, judging by the wince when I held her too tight, but she was okay. Things couldn't get much worse. From here, it could only get better.

The bedroom door hinges squealed, calling my attention that way. Declan leaned against the frame, looking a mess. His hair wasn't brushed, his wide eyes were framed by deep, dark circles, and the armpits of his white T-shirt were doused in sweat. "Good. You're awake."

"Barely." Pulling away from Ria, I stretched my arms overhead. "Did you sleep on the couch?"

"Didn't get much sleep at all, actually. And you need to wake up. Pretty damn fast. Because we got a problem. A problem I have no idea how to handle, but I'm pretty sure you do, you little fucking psychopath."

Brows furrowing, I crossed my arms against my chest. "Well, fuck you, too."

Massaging his forehead, he blew out a deep breath. "I say that with love. Really, I do. Because right now, that's what I need. My little fucking psychopath. We gotta go. Like, ten minutes ago, we got to go."

"Are the cops here or something?" Ria asked.

Standing from the bed, I caught a glimpse of some red on Declan's fingers.

"No. I really hope not, anyway." He looked over Ria for a moment, then said, "You... You should probably stay here."

"What? Why?" she asked.

"What is that?" I squinted at Declan's hands. "Jesus Christ, did you kill somebody?"

"No. No, I did not. But... Well, *I*, I did not."

Mangled wasn't the right word for this. Davey, the drug dealer I'd met yesterday, the one who was apparently pimping out my sister, was almost unidentifiable. All that I recognized was the tattoo on his wrist. His face? Hardly more than a pile of mush.

Declan was a few feet from the body, squatting, propping his elbows on his knees and holding his hands over his mouth and nose. Of all people here, he should have been the least bothered by this. But the stereotypes surrounding Werewolves were clearly just that.

With tight lips, Emory stood beside the pile of mush that must've been Davey's brain a few hours prior. I wouldn't have described his expression as casual, but he was certainly less panicked than Declan.

"You did this?" I asked.

Emory spared me a glance, then nodded.

"Bare hands?" I asked.

He dug in the pocket of his blood speckled jeans and held up a pair of brass knuckles. Not brass, though. Silver. Certainly an effective way to take on a Vampire. I preferred knives, but to each their own.

"What the hell were you thinking?" I asked. "Was it your plan to come here and kill him? Because you realize how much this fucks things up for Declan, right? Now we have no one to pin Alicia's murder on. How the fuck are we going to plant evidence anywhere to point it back to the person who actually did the damn thing when he's fucking dead, Emory?"

"At least I was smart enough to bring him out here." Emory gestured around the yard.

And for that, I did have to give him credit. It was better he killed him out here than in there. A crime scene in the elements was easier to cover up than one inside a home.

"Yeah, except for the fact that mine and Declan's DNA is all over the inside of that place." I pointed to the old Victorian. "Jesus Christ. Why dd you do this?"

"Why do you think?" Suddenly, his eyes were venomous, his voice just as lethal. "What he did to Ria. You're not stupid, right? You put two and two together. What? Am I the bad guy here for killing a murderous, raping, piece of shit?"

Slowly, my stomach dropped. "He…"

"Maybe," Declan said, voice hardly more than a murmur. "She wouldn't talk about it. But I smelled something on her, and when she was getting in the car, she was in a skirt, and I saw more of her than I wanted to." Still, his voice was hardly audible, and he simply stared at the mauled carcass on the grass. "Probably something she should talk to you about anyway. But, yeah, it looks like that was what happened."

As sick as that made me, I didn't have time to process it. Right now, we needed to fix this. Or do our best to.

But, if I was being honest, that wasn't where my head went. I was more concerned with why Emory did this for Ria. He hadn't needed to. But he did. Why?

"This your first time?" I asked him.

"First time doing what?" Emory asked.

"Killing someone."

A sound that almost resembled a laugh. "You *would* be the person to ask that."

"Was it, or wasn't it?"

"It was," he said. "Why?"

Emory had faced a lot of hardship in his life. Maybe not the same as mine, but hardships all the same. And this was what had sent him over the edge? Someone beating and raping his friend? *Friend*, being the operative word in that sentence.

Something I could pick apart later, I supposed.

"Alright." Massaging my forehead, looking between the body on the ground and the house, I debated where to start. "Alright. Do you need a minute to collect yourself, baby?"

Declan glanced up, then dropped back onto his ass, looking unusually green. "Just... Just give me five."

"Well, you might want to take your five over there." I pointed to the tree line. "Because, Emory, you got a knife on you?"

He lifted a pocket knife from his jeans. "Like this?"

"No, not like that." Rubbing my eyes, I exhaled deeply. "We need Ria. Go grab her."

"You really think she should see this?" Emory asked.

"I think she should've been the one to fucking kill him," I snapped. "But you took that from her. Because you think she's such a sensitive little flower that doesn't know how to take care of herself. I assure you, she does. But that doesn't matter right now. I need her for the spells. So go get her."

He tightened his jaw at that, but he disappeared.

"Why don't I want to see this?" Declan asked.

"Given the fact that you seem to be a little squeamish today, you don't want to see how gory this is going to get."

Even from here, I could hear his stomach gurgle. "How gory *is* it going to get?"

"Well, I'll burn his body. But we need his hand first."

Blinking hard a few times, Declan lifted a hand over his mouth. "What do you mean 'you need his hand?'"

"I mean, your job is going be going through the house and sniffing out our scents. Then we're gonna wipe all the surfaces that we touched, which is a lot. And then, I'm gonna go through with Davey's amputated hand and put his fingerprints on everything. So that it doesn't look like it was staged."

Entirely involuntarily, he gagged.

I loved that about him. My cruelty disgusted him. It was better than the reverse. Someone completely unbothered by these things wouldn't be my type. And no, the irony of that wasn't lost on me.

"I'm giving you the easy job," I said. "But if you know another Werewolf who could help us faster—"

"I'm fine." The bile I felt burning his esophagus said otherwise. "We don't want to get anybody else involved with this. Let's just clean it up and call it a day. Then we can figure out how to keep me out of jail."

"Maybe we can hold on to the hand," I murmured. "If I cauterize it, I could, in theory, take it with me into the police department and put it on pieces of evidence from the murder scene. Or, the dump scene, I guess. Then, in theory, it would tie everything to him, and there would be nothing leading back to you. And that's what we need, right? Hard evidence."

Nose wrinkled, lips curled, Declan shook his head. "I love you, sweetheart, and I love that you know how to handle this shit, because I sure as hell don't. But you can leave me out of the details."

I almost smiled at that, but Ria and Emory landed at my side before I had any time to respond.

Gradually, as Ria looked at the ground, her jaw fell open. Not with disgust, but shock. After a long, quiet moment, she looked up at Emory. "You did this?"

"I'm sorry." His voice was so much softer when he talked to her. "I don't know what I came here for. I just saw you coming into the house, looking like this"—he gestured over her—"and I lost it. I just... I lost it."

As if he was her high school date who had just arrived at the door with a bouquet of roses and a limo, she smiled up at him. "Don't apologize."

"We have to get this done. ASAP. It won't be long, and people are gonna be coming here to get their drugs," I said.

"Right," Ria said. "What you need from me?"

"Well, I need his hands. Left and right." I gestured to them. "You brought a knife, right?"

She reached into her hoodie pocket, and pulled out a six-inch blade. One of my athames, which I used for ceremonies, and felt very dirty about using for a purpose like this. But time was of the essence. "Think this'll work?"

"With the arm he's got on him?" I hooked a thumb toward Emory. "Yeah, shouldn't be a problem."

He rolled his eyes at me, then reached for the blade.

But Ria pulled it back. "You killed him. I get this."

I imagined that would be the last I ever heard of what Davey did to her. Ria was as emotionally walled up as I was. Sure, she was sweet, but we buried shit. Aside from when we were under the influence, we didn't acknowledge what our trauma had done to us. If we swept it under the rug, even we couldn't see it.

It was how we coped. And if that's how she got through this? Along with chopping off his hands? The hands that had violated her in more ways than I could ever know? Well, so be it. Who was I to judge?

Emory gave a curt nod.

I turned to Declan. "Ready to go clean up?"

Struggling up onto his knees, then taking my hand for support as he stood the rest of the way up, he said, "If it means I don't have to watch this man's hands get hacked off, yes. Yes, please."

CHAPTER TWENTY-TWO

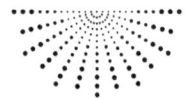

DECLAN

The smell of human flesh burning.

It was something I could've gone my whole life without knowing. Of course, that was only the smell of Ria cauterizing the wounds from where she sawed off Davey's hands. I didn't even want to know how bad it would be when she burned the whole body.

But I had a job to do. While Ria and Emory tended to Davey, Brooke and I got to work inside the old house. We used one another's memories to remember exactly what we had touched, then wiped every surface. If we were smart, we would've worn gloves yesterday. But we had figured that we were dealing with drug dealers. We hadn't thought that we would be committing, or covering up, a murder here.

"Why do you think Emory did this?" Brooke asked, wiping a large shard of one of the bongs she had shattered yesterday afternoon. I didn't know how she expected to get her fingerprints off of all the pieces, but she was attempting. At least she was wearing gloves this time.

"Because he lost his shit?" Leaning toward the sofa, I sniffed. Sure enough, one of Brooke's long, curly red hairs laid against the back of the cushion. "I mean, when I saw Ria like that, I was ready to come in here and kill him too. Don't know if I would've done it the way he did, but, yeah. I get it."

"Why didn't you?" she asked. "You could have. You didn't. He did. Why?"

Straightening, dropping Brooke's hair into a Ziploc bag, I shrugged. "I don't know. Didn't feel like it was my place."

"Right." Standing, she propped her hands on her hips. "And yet, he thought it was his place. Why?"

"I think you're trying to get at something here, but it's not computing. Just explain."

She crossed her arms against her chest. "Ria and Emory, they're close. They're good friends. Right?"

"Right..."

"Would you kill someone like that for a good friend?"

I paused, cocking my head to the side. "In the heat of the moment. I did for you, and I barely knew you then."

"Right. But that was the heat of the moment. He hurt me, you saw it, and you lost your temper. And I'm not shaming him for this. It was justice. If Emory hadn't done this, I would've come back and done it myself. If Ria didn't want to, at least."

"There's a point here that you're trying to make, and it's completely going over my head."

"It wasn't the heat of the moment," she said. "He had time to think before he did it, and he did it anyway. He didn't even know for sure if this was the guy, right? Because he didn't see it happen. But he still did it."

"Yeah, sweetheart, we established that he did it." My tone surely expressed my annoyance this time. "Get to the point."

"I mean, they spend time together literally every day. They practically live up each other's asses. And I just thought it was because they were best friends, but you wouldn't do this for a best friend. You'd get angry over a best friend getting hurt, but you wouldn't completely lose your shit and kill someone for the first time in your life. If you've done it before, if you work for the Chambers or something, maybe I can see it happening. But he hasn't. He's never had to defend himself like this. He didn't need to defend *her* like that. But he did. So why? Why did he do it unless he's in love with her?"

Brows raising, I crossed my arms and leaned against the edge of the sofa. "Shit."

"Exactly my point."

"But he's gay."

"Are you sure he's not bi?"

"I've only ever seen him with guys, so I don't think so."

"Look, he's your friend," she said. "But you should ask him."

"Or, we could mind our business."

"Ria *is* my business." She shot me a look. "She told me this morning that she wants to go to rehab. She'll probably be in for thirty or sixty days, maybe ninety if we can find her a good bed. When she gets out, if she's serious about this, she's gonna be in a really fragile state. Losing her best friend because he has feelings for her, and she doesn't feel the same way, could break her. Or vice versa. Say he has feelings but decides he can't deal with an addict. Not that I don't understand, but that'd the crush her. I want her to get it together and keep it together. So if you don't talk to him, I'm going to."

I frowned. That was fair. And it'd probably sound better coming from me. "Alright. I'll talk to him. What do you want me to say? Don't hurt her? Don't break her heart? Or leave her alone completely?"

Brooke got quiet for a moment, no longer wiping her fingerprints off of the baseball bat she had wrecked the house with yesterday afternoon. After a few heartbeats, she met my gaze. "They really are best friends."

"They are," I agreed.

"If I could pick anyone for my little sister, it would be someone like Emory. He's a good guy. He has his shit together. He drinks, but not a whole lot, and he doesn't really do drugs." She paused, thinking, lowering herself to sit on the sofa. "Tell him that if he's gonna do anything, if he's gonna pursue her, it can't be until she has some clean time under her belt. Six months at least. Preferably longer, but at least six months. That sounds fair, doesn't it?"

Giving a sad smile, I nodded. "I think so."

She smiled too, but it was just as sad as mine. "I hope she does. Get clean, I mean. She's the best person when she's sober. She's the best person, period. But I just don't want her to end up in a situation like this again. I want what's best for her, you know?"

Peeling off my gloves, I reached out to cup her cheek. "I do know."

Her cheeks turned bright red. "What else do you know?"

Shy. She looked so shy, bashful, and adorable from down there. Looking up at me like this. We stood about the same height, so I didn't get to feel bigger than her often. After last night though, I realized that was exactly the case. It may have been a rare occasion for me to notice it, but she looked up to me every day. She relied on me. But for a moment, I really felt it.

"What do you mean?" I asked, thumbing her chin.

"What did I say to you last night?" she asked. "I don't remember it. I vaguely remember getting drunk at Spades. Kinda remember you helping me shower?" Her cheeks burned brighter at that last bit. "But I don't remember much else."

"You told me you love me." I smiled when I said that, and her smile dropped. Not like she was ashamed, but like she was embarrassed. This next part would only embarrass her more. "You told me why it's so hard for you to say that. 'I love you,' I mean. And I get it now. It was nice to hear it, but you don't have to say it again. If it's too hard for you, I understand. I'll settle for my, 'you too.' The occasional, 'same here.'"

Brooke laughed. "I do. You know I do, right?"

Until last night, no, I hadn't. Well, I had. Until Emory had pointed out that she never said it and made me question everything. But... "Yeah, I do."

She smiled a little bigger. "I'm gonna work on it. Talking more. Opening up to you. I know I'm not good at it, but I'm—"

Leaning in, I cut her off with a kiss. It was long, hard, and slow. Deep. Not passionate and fiery, but powerful and soothing.

When I finally pulled back, resting my forehead against hers, staring into those crystal blue eyes, I shook my head. "You don't need to. Not until you're ready. But not because I'm going anywhere, alright? It stresses me out that you don't communicate as well as I do. But I don't want you to think that I'm going anywhere. I'm not gonna leave you just because we work a little different than everybody else. I love you no matter what, sweetheart. I'm not leaving you."

I repeated that so many times to get it through her head.

It seemed to have done the trick, because her eyes twinkled with tears. Like that was exactly what she needed to hear. That I mattered as much to her she did to me. That we were both broken, and fucked up, and no good at this. We both sucked at relationships, probably because neither of us had seen healthy ones. But we would figure it out. Because this was real.

Words weren't, but this was.

After a few heartbeats, she pulled away, blinking. As if I hadn't already seen the tears. Clearing her throat, she stood. "We should hurry. We need to get that body burned ASAP."

What a wonderful ending to a beautiful moment.

CHAPTER TWENTY-THREE

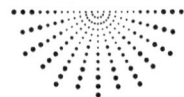

BROOKE

Over the rest of the day, we finalized the plan.

There was another car parked outside now. The one Alicia's neighbors had described with the fancy wheels. So we teleported to Alicia's house and planted a few of her belongings in it. Could they prove it was the car that was used to transport her body? No, absolutely not. But it would prove that she had, in fact, been here.

There really wasn't much that could be done about the body. It had to go, and that was that. So we burned it. Regular fire wasn't hot enough to turn a body to ash, but we were Witches. We weren't using gasoline. We used a spell, one that turned Davey's body to ash within less than ten minutes.

The longest part was waiting for the smell of burned flesh to dissipate so Declan could get a good scent and search for blood droplets. Davey's, Ria's, and Emory's. From what I could tell, Emory hadn't lost a drop. But, here we were. Making progress. Covering up a murder.

When we were finished, it was almost seven. Declan did another walk through the house, just to check again for scents. Emory and Ria looked all over for fingerprints we may have missed. Then, for good measure, we took Davey's severed hands and slathered them all over everything. Clasped the fingers around an empty glass on the countertop. The door handles. The refrigerator, the sink handle, all over the countertops, all over everything that Declan and I had touched yesterday, just to be certain that we didn't miss anything.

By eight, we were as close to certain as we could be. With a spell, we had regrown the patch of burned soil in the yard. Alicia's belongings were inside Davey's car. The dead girl was now tied to the drug dealer's—her true murderer's—house.

And with that, we did *not* got home. We went to the middle of the city and found a pay phone. The cops were now familiar with my voice, Declan's and Emory's as well, but they didn't know Ria's. So, she called the local PD and put in an anonymous tip.

"Alicia Tanner, she was my friend," she said, not having to pretend to make her voice tremble. "We worked together. On the streets, I mean. She got caught up with some guy. He started as her dealer, and then he became more than that. Her clientele became his, if you know what I mean. He didn't like when she worked without him. I think he's the one who killed her. His name's Davey Johnson." She listed the address, and then she hung up.

Walking up beside her, I rested a hand on her back. "You did good."

She did her best to form a smile. Sniffling, she cleared her throat. "Anybody down for breakfast before we start calling rehabs?"

"I'll make it," Emory said. "Let's go back to Spades."

While we ate, I scoured a few of my spell books. It wasn't the worst thing if she went to rehab looking the way she did, but if I could ease some of Ria's pain before then, that would be preferable. Sure enough, I found something just as Declan was clearing the table. I didn't have all of the ingredients on hand, so I had to teleport back to my house to grab them.

But, within an hour, Ria was almost back to normal, awaiting a ride from the rehab center at 5 PM. Her lips were still a bit swollen, but the blue and black around her eyes had mostly faded. Now, they were only discolored because of the withdrawals. She still had a small cut along her forehead, but it was smaller than it had been. The boys had left the room as I finished up, so I thought it was time I addressed the bit that Declan had mentioned this afternoon. Of course, I had to ease my way into that one. "I'm so proud of you."

She smiled. "I couldn't have done it without you."

"You don't give yourself enough credit." Tucking some hair behind her ear, I returned the smile. "But once we get you checked in and everything, once we get you settled, I don't want you to end up here again."

A breathy laugh. "Believe me, neither do I."

"I don't want you to end up where you were last night again," I said, voice softer now. "Declan said he thought that it was more than just a beating. Is that true?"

Now, she avoided my gaze. When she broke the silence, I didn't know how to describe the sound she let out. A laugh? Huff? "I'm fine. Don't worry about it, Brooke."

"I am gonna worry about it." Finding her hand, I laced her fingers through mine. "It's my job to worry about you. I always will—"

"It's not your job." A pure, genuine smile. "You're supposed to be my sister. You're not supposed to be my mom. I appreciate everything that you've done for me. I appreciate that you stepped into that role when no one else was there to. But no, you don't have to worry about me. You don't have to take care of me either. And when I get out, I'd appreciate it if you didn't. Let me fall, if that's what I do, but I have to get it together on my own."

So there it was. She wasn't gonna talk about what happened last night. Probably never would. Which was fair enough. She wasn't obligated to share her story.

And she was right. Caring for her wasn't *my* job. I didn't have to do that, and it was probably best if I stopped. All I was going to do was make things worse if I kept enabling her, and maybe I had needed to hear her say that to understand it. To get it through my head, I needed her to tell me to stop.

"Fine. I'll let you fall on your face." I smiled, and she laughed. "Because no matter how much I love you, I really can't do it anymore, Ria. You have to get it together."

Pressing her lips together, she nodded. "I'm gonna."

"You better."

Another laugh. "You always were the tough love type."

"And don't you forget it." I joined in on the laughter. When it faded, Ria rested her head on my shoulder. I kissed her forehead, tucking an arm around her ribs. "Did you ask if I'm allowed to come visit you?"

Hugging me back, she gave a nod. "Not until after I'm out of detox. And then I only get two hours of in-person visitation a week for the first month. In the second month, I get two hours twice a week. And then, by the third month, I can leave. Not for the whole day, but for a couple of hours. As long as I stay in the program."

I squeezed her tight. "You *better* stay in the program."

I expected the playful nature of this conversation to continue, but she cuddled up closer to me and said, "I have to. I don't want you to lose me too."

Suddenly, I had to hold my breath to keep from crying.

She couldn't get clean for me. It had to be for herself, or it wouldn't stick. But, judging by the tears in her eyes now, I knew it wasn't just about me. It was about last night. Last night was her *I-can't-keep-living-like-this* moment.

I hated that she had to live through something like that. I hated that it happened to her. But I was glad that something had changed. That some-how, now, she had a reason to get clean. I would pray every day that it would stick. Who I was praying to was irrelevant. I wasn't sure I believed in anything outside of what I already knew to exist. But I prayed like hell, because maybe, just maybe, some god out there was listening. Maybe one of them would step up and help her get it together.

A knock at the door called my attention away. With another kiss on Ria's forehead, I stood. When I made it there, I wasn't surprised to see Detective Tyler on the other side. I glanced back at Declan, just stepping out of the hallway behind the bar. "I don't see a warrant. Want me to answer it?"

"He's not gonna go away if you don't," he said.

And so, with a sigh, I pulled it open. Like I did yesterday, I put on that big, innocent, bimbo smile—as Declan would have described it. "Hey, there, Detective. I was gonna bring my car down to the station this after-noon if that's still okay. Is there anything else I can help you with?"

Tracing his tongue along his lips, he gave a crooked smile. "Not gonna pull another disappearing act, are you?"

I cocked my head to the side. "I'm sorry?"

"I got an informant in here yesterday." He looked around the bar. Then he pointed to a chair in the center of the room. "He was sitting right there while he was wearing the camera. Not the greatest quality, but you were fighting. You two, I mean." He wagged a finger between Declan and me. "You can be a real dick, by the way. And you, you're a big fat phony, aren't you? It all makes sense now. It's *all* making sense. The drugs that the dogs would smell, then disappear as soon as we got close. The bodies that would vanish. The people we *knew* were dead, but could never find. All of these things that never made sense, now all tie together." He looked between us all. Declan, me, Ria, Emory. He looked between us, and he cackled. "You're not human. None of you are human."

CHAPTER TWENTY-FOUR

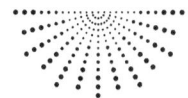

DECLAN

Before I could say another word, Emory was gone. Or rather, *not* gone.

He was behind Tyler with an arm around his throat. Then he was gone again.

Suddenly, he was in the center of the room, dragging a chair closer to the bar. All while still holding Tyler.

Shoving him down into the chair, he glanced my way. "Get some duct tape."

Tyler's mouth dropped open, and he hurled his guts out. I wasn't sure if it was intentional when his vomit wound up all over Emory's jeans or not, but I didn't have time to question.

I just stood there with my jaw on the floor. "What the fuck are you doing?"

"He's right," Brooke said. "Get the duct tape."

"What? Are we gonna kill him too?" I asked, eyes shifting rapidly around the room.

Brooke shot me a look. "Well, we can't let him run off with this. If he has evidence of our abilities, the Chambers are gonna kill him anyway."

"And since when do we side with the god damned Chambers?" Lifting both hands to my head, I grabbed fistfuls of hair. "You're gonna make this so much worse. Tying up a cop in the middle of my bar when his car's outside is a really fucking bad idea."

Ria frowned at me. "I'll get the duct tape. Where is it?"

Brooke told her, and she scurried to the utility closet in the back.

Tyler was still puking. That was common enough for people who weren't used to teleporting. It took some time to adjust to the sensation. It was like putting a child who had just eaten two funnel cakes and five corn dogs on a tilt-a-whirl. It sounded like a fun idea, and it never was.

"Who's your informant?" Emory asked, forcefully holding Tyler into the chair. He didn't seem to mind the vomit all over both of them. "Who's your CI?"

Tyler just hurled in response. The smell of it was making me want to do the same.

"Jesus Christ," I said, pressing both hands to my eyes. "This is bad. This is very, *very* bad."

"No shit, Sherlock," Brooke said. "This is bigger than us. No matter what he says, we need to talk to somebody. Someone above us. The Chambers."

"We're not getting the Chambers involved," I said. "I might hate this asshole, but I don't want them to kill him."

"Depending on who he shared that information with, killing him won't make much of a difference anyway," Brooke said. "Shit. Shit, shit, *shit*."

"Who's your CI?" Emory had Tyler's face in his hands now, squeezing so tight that I swore I heard bones cracking. "Answer the fucking question."

"How the hell is he going to answer you when you're breaking his face, man?" I snapped.

Emory didn't give me so much as a glance for that, but he did release Tyler's face. "I'm gonna give you until the count of five, and if you don't answer—"

"Mason Cooper," Tyler said. Gradually, his face screwed up. Like he didn't understand why he admitted that. Cops were never supposed to give up their CIs.

"That little fucker. I told you." I wagged a finger at Emory. "I told you I didn't want him in my god damned bar, and you said he was fine. You said he wouldn't do anything to anybody. And look at this—"

"Can we argue about this later?" Still pinning Tyler to the chair, Emory shot me the filthiest look. "A little preoccupied at the moment."

I grumbled a curse. He may not have been wrong, but he certainly wasn't right.

They were friends in high school. Emory was a few years younger than me, and I didn't know the guy personally. But Emory insisted that he was cool. I was fairly certain that it had very little to do with how cool Mason was, and a lot more to do with how good Mason was in the sack. We could argue about it later.

Ria returned with the duct tape, and Emory got straight to work tying Tyler up. But as soon as the duct tape made contact with his wrist, Tyler screamed, "Help! Somebody help—"

Suddenly, Brooke was beside Emory. Pressing her hand over Tyler's mouth, she lowered her voice to an octave I'd only heard it reach once. Yesterday, when she was torturing poor Oliver, it deepened like it did now. "I *really* don't want to kill you. Really, I don't. I have seen enough bodies today. But give me a fucking reason, Detective, and I won't have any choice. Is that what you want? Do you want me to kill you?"

With wide, unblinking eyes, Tyler sealed his lips shut. Deep breaths panted in and out of his nose instead, chest rising and falling at an impeccable speed. Cortisol wafted from him in clouds.

The man was terrified. As he should've been. If I were on the receiving end of Emory and Brooke's ferocity, I'd be terrified too.

"Who knows about this?" Emory asked. "Who did you tell?"

"No one," Tyler said. Again, confusion pinched his forehead. Damn, I did love Emory's ability to make people tell the truth.

"Where's the evidence of it?" Brooke asked.

"The original is in my office. At home, I mean." Again, Tyler tried to keep his mouth shut, but the words kept falling out. "What the hell is this? How are you making me talk? It doesn't—"

"A unique gift of mine," Emory said. "And not the point here. The original? So you made copies?"

Nodding slowly, Tyler swallowed hard. "One's in a safety deposit box in town. Another one is hidden in the air vent in my living room. I've got another one down at the station, and I buried one in the woods."

"Jesus Christ," Brooke said. "Why? Why is figuring this out so important to you?"

"This place has been connected to a thousand crimes," Tyler snarled. "Drug trafficking, murder, prostitution. I need evidence to shut the place down." His eyes turned to me. "To take *you* down."

"You wanted to take *my dad* down," I snapped. "I don't break the law.

Or at least, not often. I don't deal drugs, I don't get sex that's paid for, and I don't..." Scratching my head, I stopped myself before I could lie.

"But you do kill people?" he asked.

"Like you haven't killed people," I said. "Don't look at me like that. I kill people when I have to. And they fucking deserved it. Has every person you've shot deserved it?"

"I didn't kill a hooker—"

Emory smacked him across the face.

"Fuck!" Tyler's daggers of eyes turned up to Emory. "What was that for?!"

"I don't like that word," Emory said.

"But he does," Ria said, crossing her arms and leaning against the bar, facing the two of them with her back to me. "I know this guy. Didn't know he was a cop on this case, but I do know him. He's never bought my services, but I've seen him with a few friends."

Again, Emory slapped him across the face

"Jesus!" Tyler yelled.

"Well, maybe I wouldn't have hit you if you weren't a raging hypocrite," Emory said.

"That's a good thing, isn't it?" Ria asked Brooke. "If he's out on the corner getting his dick sucked by girls like me, we can use that against him. Blackmail?"

"Blackmail isn't gonna cut it," Brooke said, shaking her head. "He knows way too much. And he's a cop. Who're we gonna turn him into? The other cops who also get their dicks sucked by girls like you?"

"Touché," Ria murmured.

"Memory manipulation," Emory said. "He smells like booze, and it's— What? Ten o'clock? We can make him think he was on a drunken bender for the last week. Erase all this."

"Too risky," Brooke said. "I can fuck with his head, but I'll miss things. I'm a Witch, not a Fae. A Fae might be able to pull it off, but I leave one string dangling, he'll pull on it, and the whole charade'll come falling down. The walls I build in his mind will crumble. No, we need help."

"Don't say the Chambers," I said.

Brooke rolled her eyes at me, then snatched her purse off the table. Gesturing to Emory, she said, "Be ready to move him. Know any abandoned warehouses? Sketchy caves? Anyone knocks on that door, take him there."

She turned to me. "If he gets out, you get him back in that chair."

154

She looked at Ria. "And you get his car outta here. Somewhere it won't be found. Put the closed sign on the door on your way out."

"And where the hell are you going?" I called after her down the hall.

She held her cellphone—the disposable one—in the air. "Trying to save all our fucking asses!"

CHAPTER TWENTY-FIVE

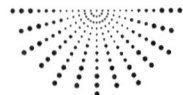

BROOKE

"Pick up. Pick up, pick up, *pick up*," I murmured, bouncing with anticipation. I glanced around the corner of the bar at the adjacent roadway, waiting for the cavalry. A dozen police cruisers, maybe an ambulance. Hell, maybe a fire truck.

"If this is about that trouble your boyfriend's into—"

"Thank gods." Breathing out a sigh of relief, I clasped a hand over my heart. "Genevieve."

"Something's wrong. Of course it is. You only call when something's wrong. Just like the rest of you."

"You want to get coffee sometime?"

"I prefer tea." She paused. "But this is business, I'm assuming."

"If you want to call it that, sure. Business. Or, a massive exposure risk."

"Oh, bloody hell." I could practically hear her rubbing her temples. "What is it?"

"Are you on a protected line?"

"I'll call you back on one."

And so, she did. Almost every call I made to Genevieve, I used my disposable phone for. That was why she knew it was me when I called.

I explained the situation, ending with, "Do you know anyone who can help? Someone powerful enough to help me erase the last week from his mind? Or, maybe even a Fae. They're good at this. They could fix this in a heartbeat, right?"

Again, another deep sigh echoed through the speaker. "Well, I'm really not sure if you're ready, but if they get mad at me for this, I'm blaming you. Both of you. And Emory. And your little sister. You all are taking the blame for this. And you better tell them so, do you understand me? Because I do not want to hear it from them. Especially Jeremy. I do love when he talks mean to me, but—"

"Jesus Christ, Genevieve," I snapped. "Do you know someone or not?"

"Quite testy for someone who's in such dire need of help."

"Well, forgive me. I'm a little bit worried we're all about to end up in some CIA testing facility where they try to map our genomes and duplicate our abilities and—"

Genevieve cut me off with a laugh. "The CIA will do no such thing. Do you have a pen and paper, darling?"

I didn't have any paper, but I had a pen in my purse. After finding it in the rubble, I said, "Go ahead."

She stated an address ending with, "It's not far from Minneapolis, Minnesota."

Breaths stopping in my chest, my heart pumped faster. "But that's a day's drive. I've never even been to Minnesota. Do they know I'm coming? Should you maybe let them know?"

"Believe me, when they see you two, they'll know you. Just tell them about your dreams. The memories, I mean," Genevieve said. "And I'll drop you a crystal. Should land on the bar at Spades. That'll give you a clear enough image of the place so you can teleport there."

Well, that was much more feasible. "Okay. Okay, thank you. Thank you so much."

"You owe me far more than a thank you," Genevieve said. "But don't forget that I warned you. I'm really not sure if you're ready for what you're about to learn. But, you got yourself into this mess, and I don't know how to get you out of it. And I'm sorry, but I can't keep playing these silly games. They can handle you from here on."

I had no idea what that meant, and there was no point in stressing about it. Not right now. If they could help, they were who I was asking for.

"Either way. Thank you."

Genevieve started to say something else, but I had already flipped the phone shut and started inside. I was barely halfway down the hall when a clunk sounded, followed by Declan yelling, "Jesus Christ."

Sure enough, when I made it to the end of the hall, stepping into the dining area, there it was. A little gem, clear in color, laying on the center of the bar.

"She might be a bitch, but she always pulls through for us," I said, jogging to the little rock. "When we get there, our line is that Genevieve told us they could help us understand the memories I keep seeing."

"Genevieve." Declan was still tense from the jolt of the teleporting crystal when I met his gaze. "Of course. It's always Genevieve who does weird shit like open a little portal in the middle of my bar and drop a crystal through it." He paused. "Wait, this is something to do with the par animarum?"

"Hell if I know. That's just what Genevieve said. And she told me to warn you that we were not ready for this, but we don't have another choice." Grabbing his hand from his side, I snatched the crystal off the counter. "So, fingers crossed we don't hate ourselves after this."

Declan said something, but I paid him no mind.

When I held the crystal in my palm, focused on the energy inside of it, I saw a memory. Genevieve's memory, judging by the reflection in a car driving past.

From what I could tell, it was a small town. Little businesses stacked beside one another, leaving very few alleys in between. The business she stood before, however, did have one. The memory wasn't clear enough to make out the name on the sign, but the red brick, the pleasant white awnings, the pretty blue sky overhead gave me a clear enough depiction of where I was headed.

What I focused on, however, was that little alley beside it. Specifically, the dumpster.

"Hang on," I said to Declan.

"I hate my life," he muttered.

———

"Where the hell are we?" Declan asked, tilting his head back to look around. When he straightened, his foot collapsed into something, and he sniffed. Darting eyes turned on me, he snapped, "A fucking dumpster, Brooke?"

"Better than the middle of a busy street." Struggling up on a bag of something that smelled both disgusting and delicious, rotting food mixed with coffee, I gripped the metal frame for stability. "You should jump out, and then tell me if the coast is clear so I can teleport out."

He glared. "You're serious."

"Sure, we can both jump out. But I'm a lady. You obviously are not. So I see no harm in you jumping out of the dumpster. I might look a little bit ridiculous."

Tightening his jaw, he rolled his eyes. "Hate you. I hate you, so fucking much."

And yet, he was climbing out of the dumpster. When his feet hit the cement outside, he grunted, "Coast is clear."

So, I teleported to his side.

"Where is this dumpster located?"

Dusting the debris off my pants, I fixed my blouse. "Minnesota."

"Minnesota. Sure. Makes perfect sense," he said under his breath. "And what's in Minnesota?"

"Jeremy, I think Guinevere said. But she also said 'they,' so I'm assuming it's more than just Jeremy."

Again, his jaw clenched tightly. I wasn't sure if it was because of the little bit of information we had, or the fact that I mentioned another man. God forbid we ever need somebody other than the strong, almighty Declan.

"Just... Stay cool in there, alright?" Declan said. "If we don't know what we're walking into, we should be careful."

As if I needed Declan to tell me twice. But, to save ourselves from an argument, I just agreed and carried on around the bend and inside.

I didn't know what I was expecting, but it wasn't this. A quaint, cozy café in a cute little town. One with green walls, dark wood flooring, and an almost familial vibe. There was a man a decade or so my senior at a stage in the corner with two toddlers. The stage was nothing fancy, barely enough to fit one person and a guitar, but there was equipment there, suggesting someone did, in fact, play music here.

On the far right was the checkout counter. There was a pastry case, a fancy espresso machine, and a thousand pretty desserts inside. Behind that checkout counter stood a pretty barista. With her dark hair pulled back into a high ponytail, I couldn't tell how long it was. But what stood out about her were the vines and flowers covering much of her visible skin. Although she didn't have any tattoos on her face, her neck and arms were covered in them, hardly any pale white flesh showing. And even from here, just approaching while she looked the opposite direction, her bright green eyes stood out like emeralds in a sea of rubies.

Green eyes like that were unachievable in nature. Human nature, anyway. As I got closer, when I saw her in more detail, I was sure of it. Not only that she was Fae, but I knew what Guinevere meant now when she said to tell her about my memories.

When she said all of you, that I could be their problem now, when she said I wasn't ready for this, she didn't mean that I wasn't ready to meet this woman. She meant that I wasn't ready for the information she would have.

Because now, as I looked at her, I knew exactly who she was.

In the memories, she had a name. One I hadn't remembered until I looked into those green eyes.

"Excuse me," I said.

She turned our way, hopping off the stool behind the bar. I hadn't realized how short she was. The stool had made it look like she was standing, but she couldn't have been more than 5'5". "I'm sorry. Didn't hear you come in. What can I get you?"

"Um," I murmured, squinting her over, making sure that I wasn't about to spout something I'd regret. After all, I didn't feel a supernatural energy signature coming off her, but she knew Guinevere, who could certainly conceal that.

"Caramel macchiato and a black coffee." Declan dropped some money on the counter. "Are you the owner?"

"I am, yep." Fiddling behind the register, she kept giving that familiar smile. She didn't look the *same* as she did in the memories. Her face was rounder, nose softer, lips smaller, but it was unmistakable. The girl in the dreams and the girl who stood before me had to have been the same people. "Why do you ask?"

"Um," I said, apparently being the only word I remembered at the moment. Eventually, I managed to spit out, "Do you know Guinevere?"

Pouring a coffee behind the register, she cocked her head to the side. "Not off the top of my head. Why do you ask?"

Her demeanor had shifted, the friendly, customer service voice was starting to fade out into something a little more defensive. "She, uh... She said you could help us."

Slowly setting the coffee onto the counter, she squinted at me, and then at Declan. Her eyes came back to me, and the faintest hint of a smile teased the corner of her lips. "Oh, yeah? With what?

"Make sense of the things we're seeing," Declan answered. "Are you familiar with the phrase par animarum?"

That hint of a smile stretched a mile wide. "I am *very* familiar with that phrase." This time, when she said it, there was only joy in her voice. "Why do you ask?"

"We..." I knew we had a man tied up back home and everything, but if Guinevere was right, and this was another one of us, she could answer so many questions. She could make so much of the last two years make sense. "We think we are..."

"And you're stuttering because I look like someone you know from these 'things' you're seeing."

Partially fueled by joy, partially terrified to ruin this moment with why we were really here, all I managed out was, "Kind of."

"What was her name?"

"Véa. I called her Véa."

Suddenly, the woman on the other side of the counter beamed like a little kid. "Do you remember yours?"

I almost responded, but behind her, coming through the hall to the kitchen, was a man. A man I remembered from those memories.

One I knew before I had met Drogo. One I had grown up with. One I had watched become the man who stood before me now. Only, he was different too.

His long black hair was tucked in a bun behind his head, so I could see his ears. In those memories, they had been pointed. Then, he was an elf, or at least part elf. But his bright blue eyes hadn't changed a bit. Neither had that strong jaw, big nose, and thick lips. Those lips that stretched into a smile as wide as the woman's behind the bar. "Fuck, you look so much like you used to."

I couldn't help it. For some reason, talking to him, looking at him, felt like traveling back in time. Suddenly, I was in that igloo with the hot spring, the one with the algae that turned bright colors, and I was barely old enough to leave the house alone, but I was with him, and another girl with hair just as white as her skin, and a dark-skinned, brown-eyed girl with the sweetest smile. We were dipping our toes in the water, and it was so cold everywhere else, but the four of us were in that hot spring, and everything was right with the world. It didn't matter how cold it was out there, because we were so warm in that igloo.

And the memory flashed, and suddenly, it was just him and I. That boy with the pointed ears was sitting with me in a grand room. Don't ask me to describe it—I couldn't if I tried. Because that wasn't what mattered about the memory. What mattered was, we couldn't have been more than ten, he had something in his lap that almost resembled a guitar, and I was plucking the strings on an instrument that I could best describe as a harp, but unlike any I'd seen in my current reality. And we were playing, and we sounded magnificent. Like angels.

"Nix?"

Laughing, he jogged around the woman at the counter. "Anise."

I hadn't even taken time to notice the man behind him, but now I did. And another memory flashed. He looked like Drogo. He looked like Drogo in the memory, and he looked a bit like him in the modern world, but there were differences. Most notably that Drogo was a bit more fit than that man. I didn't remember his name, though. I remembered admiring him. I remembered loving his smile. That looking at him felt like home. That it was warm and safe. That *he* was warm and safe, and I cared about him on the deepest level.

"That means..." the man said.

"You're Drogo," the woman said to Declan, smiling still.

"Declan, actually." He glanced at me. "And she's Brooke."

And suddenly, while I was still staring at the man on the other side of the counter, who I only just now realized was holding a small child, Nix wrapped his arms around me in a bear hug. He was only a few inches taller than me, probably somewhere around 6'4", but he hoisted me off the ground and spun me in a circle.

As I laughed, and he did too, this almost indescribable feeling washed through me.

Like my entire life, I had been walking in place. Stagnant. More times than I could admit, than I *dared* to admit, I was miserable. I was lonely. All I had was my baby sister, and I had nobody to help me with her. I was a parent when I had never asked to be, and I had no one else.

But suddenly, out of nowhere, I got smacked with community. That was the only way to describe this. Sisterhood. Sure, the guy who was spinning me in the circle was a man, but I felt with him how I did with my sister. The same was true for the man with the toddler on his hip. Family, but deeper than that. A connection like I had only ever felt with Declan, without the romantic or sexual attraction.

Like I belonged.

As Nix set me down, I got a peek at Declan. He was also embraced in a bear hug by the man from the memories whose name I didn't remember.

But in those memories, they looked eerily similar. In this one, all they shared was race. Indigenous descent. But then, they had been family. Brothers, maybe?

Still hugging me close, in my ear, Nix whispered, "Cousins. They were cousins."

He remembered. He read my mind, which I did not like, but he remembered.

Before I could pull back to look at him, another crash slammed into my side. The girl, from the other side of the bar. Her arms were around me, and she was squeezing, and I couldn't breathe, but it was the best feeling I had felt in so long.

I wasn't alone. For the first time in so long, I wasn't alone.

Eventually pulling back, the girl smiled up at me. "You're taller now."

"Or you're shorter." I smiled back, but it wasn't the warm smile I'd given a moment prior, because I was really beginning to struggle to breathe. "That's who you are? Véa?"

"That's who I was." Finally releasing me, enabling Nix to do the same, she gestured to the counter. "Let's get something to eat and catch up. Baby, put the closed sign on the door. And I go by Laila now, by the way."

CHAPTER TWENTY-SIX

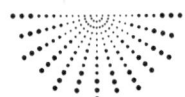

DECLAN

"Hm." Crossing his arms, Nix, who I now knew was Jeremy, leaned back in his seat. The same guy who lifted my girlfriend off the ground and spun her in a circle like they were in some sort of Hallmark movie just moments ago. "So you guys didn't come to catch up. Just here to see what we can do for you."

"Sorry," Brooke murmured. It almost sounded like she meant it, too. When she told me she was sorry, there was always a hint of sarcasm, but with these people, she felt right at home. Like she did when she was spending time with Ria.

Which I supposed made sense. Telepathically, she had told me that Jeremy had been one of her childhood best friends in the dreams she had been having. In fairness, there didn't seem to be any attraction on either of their parts, but damn it. With almost no thought, no effort, she connected with him in a way she never had with me, and I couldn't pretend like I wasn't jealous of that.

Then again, maybe she had more room to be jealous than I did. Because the guy who had picked me up in a bear hug—which was really saying something—hadn't left my side either. We were seated at a booth in a corner of the restaurant, and his knee was flush with mine. Brooke was on my right, and on the other side of the table, were Laila and Jeremy. Each of them bounced a toddler on their knee, and the guy on my right, Wyatt, had one on his, too.

Which was bizarre. I didn't know anyone with kids, and they kept looking at me. What was I supposed to say to the little shits?

This was bizarre.

The strangest part of it was the fact that I understood why Brooke felt so familial with these people. Because I wasn't the slightest bit bothered by this stranger's knee against mine. The child staring at me was another story, but the guy was sitting so close, he was almost in my lap, and... it felt natural.

I wasn't much of a touchy-feely person, but I kinda liked it. Not in a sexual way, of course, but in the sense that it felt... like home. Sitting beside him felt like sitting beside Emory.

"Cousins," Laila said, giving me a smile. She gestured between me and Wyatt. "You two were cousins. More like brothers, really. Your mom, she took him in when he was a baby, so you guys were raised as siblings."

"Can we stay on topic?" Jeremy asked. "They committed a murder today, and they've got a cop tied up in their restaurant."

"Bar, actually," Brooke said. "Technically, *we* didn't commit murder. We just covered it up."

"Hey, I am one-hundred percent cool with not changing the topic," Wyatt said, playfully elbowing me in the ribs. He had a smile that was half boyish, half contagious. "So you don't remember that at all?"

I tried to smile back. That was the friendly thing to do. But this was fucking weird. All I could do was shake my head.

Wyatt didn't seem to care. That big smile, those warm brown eyes, and his matching brown skin were all so familiar, they triggered something, some urge to open up, but no memories. I may have been uncomfortable, but so far, I was enjoying his company. "That's okay. The memories will come with time. It wasn't until—What was it? Almost two years ago now? A year and a half or so, we'll go with that. That's when I got my memories. It's eye-opening, but no need to rush anything. We've all got time."

"Topic." Jeremy's voice was firm, eyes shifting around the table. "Let's stay on it."

"Jeremy's right." Standing, Laila lifted the toddler to her hip. A little blonde boy, which was odd given the fact that they were both brunettes. "I'll go get to work. Find someone to watch the kids, would you?"

Jeremy stood as well, situating the napping toddler better in his arm—

a little girl, this one looking like she did belong to both of them—and struggled the other one into his free arm. "Yeah, you're needed more than I am anyway."

"And I am *not* needed," Wyatt said. "Put those two in the game room in the back, and I'll watch them while you're gone." He turned to me, giving that big smile again. "But you, sir, we're getting a drink tonight."

"At Spades," Brooke said. She returned that smile, and my god, it was the strangest thing.

Suddenly, she was like a whole other person. There was a certain softness in her demeanor, everything from the way that she talked, to the way that she held herself, changed in a blink. It wasn't that dramatized show she had put on for Detective Tyler yesterday. It was natural.

Was this what she had been like then? When we fell in love for the first time, was she softer than I knew her to be now? Was that why there was so often tension in our relationship this time around?

"After we get this all handled," Brooke said, "come over tonight. I'll pay."

Wyatt smiled back. "I'll bring your best friend."

Brooke cocked her head to the side.

"Celena. That's her name now," he said. "You might remember her as Luna. White blonde hair, pale blue eyes, your best bud since diapers?"

Slowly, Brooke's eyes widened. "Luna. That makes you… Rion, right?"

Smiling wider, Wyatt nodded. "The one and only."

I didn't understand. A week ago, she had told me that she only remembered flashes. Now, she knew all of their names? After that dream the other night, I knew that she remembered mine and hers. Drogo and Anise, but she knew all of these people suddenly?

Was it because she was a Witch? Was that why she remembered things that I didn't? Was it coming here, meeting them? Was that what drew out the memories?

"Alright, time is of the essence here," Laila said. "Let's move, people."

When we landed at Spades, everyone was exactly where we left them. Ria looked worse than she had earlier. Of course, she was mostly healed, but the withdrawals were clearly doing a number on her. Pacing the room, she held a hand over her belly and smelled of vomit and diarrhea, which, yes, did smell differently than Tyler's.

Emory stood against the table in front of Tyler, arms crossed with deep dark circles beneath his eyes. No worse than Ria's, though.

Tyler was still duct taped to the chair, but now, there was a piece of duct tape over his lips as well.

Making a *tsk, tsk, tsk* noise, Laila walked toward him. "You ever heard the phrase, 'put a sock in it?'"

Ria squinted, but stayed quiet.

Emory, on the other hand, said, "Who the fuck is this?"

Laila turned his way, giving a smile and letting her eyes glow. A trait that had always fascinated me about Fae. That didn't last long though. The longer she looked at him, the faster the glow burned out. Maybe *looked* wasn't the right word. She studied him. Studied him like he was in ancient painting, and she was taking in every detail. Then she looked at Ria in the same, careful way.

"Laila," Brooke said, "is apparently another one of us."

"One of you?" Ria asked. "Like, more paired souls?"

"The originals." Still watching Ria closely, Laila smiled. "And you are...?"

"My sister," Brooke answered. "Ria, meet Laila, Laila, meet Ria, and that's Emory. He's half to blame for this."

"Are you to blame for this?" Laila gestured to the duct tape over Tyler's mouth.

"Yeah?" Emory's expression showed just how unhappy he was with his work being critiqued. "He wouldn't shut up. What else would I was I supposed to do?"

"Put a sock in it." Propping her hands on her hips, Laila flapped her lips together in a trill. "Now he's going to have marks. I'm going to have to heal them. Otherwise, he'll have a rash on his face, and it's gonna blow the rest of the plan. Just for future reference, in a situation like this, where you're trying to wipe someone's memories, you don't want to leave marks behind. Makes it more complicated."

Emory glanced at her, and then at me. As if to say, *Who does this bitch think she is?*

"Oh," Ria murmured. "Yeah, I guess that does make sense."

"Still, shouldn't be too hard to heal. But I'm gonna need you boys to hold him down so I can handle them. It's gonna hurt."

"You can do both?" Ria asked. "Heal him and erase his mind?"

"I can do it all, baby," she said, smiling a bit wider. For having such a round, innocent face, there was something slightly terrifying about the way she said that. "But both of those are Spirit abilities. So, yeah. I can do both."

"Wait," I said, "does that mean you're Elite?"

Laila propped her hands on her hips. "I'm surprised you can't smell it."

She smelled... peculiar. Unlike anything I had ever smelled before. Like a delicacy from some strange corner of the universe.

"Elite Fae, a quarter Guardian, and half Angel. A bit of a mutt, I am." Again, she smiled. She seemed to do that quite a bit. It wasn't just friendly, not only familiar and familial, but almost mothering. Not like *my* mother, but that was the only word for it. Somehow playful at the same time. "And, as established, we can catch up later. Let's get the duct tape off him and clean up you guys' mess."

Shit, Elite Fae. That was rare. It meant she was descended from all five blood lines and had power over all five elements. Fire, water, air, earth, and spirit.

Just as I started toward them, Jeremy landed on the other side of the room. And the moment he did, I watched his breath stop in his chest. He wasn't looking at the detective tied to a chair, or at me, for Brooke, or at his wife. He was looking at Ria. And I swore, for half a second, there were tears in his eyes. His eyes, those bright blue eyes, stayed locked on her for far too long. Far longer than I would've been comfortable with if not for the fact that when his eyes turned on Emory, they did the exact same thing. A hint of a smile even pulled at the corners of his lips.

And it didn't take long to put it together.

He knew them. So did Laila. From another lifetime, another world, they knew them, just as they knew Brooke and me.

Were Emory and Ria like us too? Were the two of them also paired souls? That was all that made sense, and I planned to ask it. Later, when we had that drink, I planned to ask *so* many questions.

"Oh, good, you're here." Laila looked at Jeremy over her shoulder. "You got any recommendations on how we should keep him in place while I heal any marks they left without causing any more?"

Blinking a few times, Jeremy turned to me. "You got any bondage equipment?"

My brows creased. "Excuse me?"

"You were into that, once upon a time," Jeremy said. "My kinks stayed the same. I'm assuming yours did too. And the safest way to bind someone is using bondage equipment. The least likely to leave any marks."

Brooke laughed.

I did not, but I couldn't pretend I wasn't sorta fascinated. Starting toward the door, I said, "I'll be right back."

It was hard to believe how quickly they worked, but over the next five hours, our problems were solved.

Every single one of them.

Sure enough, Jeremy was right. We tied up Tyler in my fuzzy bondage straps, Laila healed him, and then she wiped his mind.

That was on the most accurate descriptor. She didn't erase it all. She just... warped it. At least, that was my understanding. I didn't know many Fae, nor how their abilities worked. Actually, I'd only met a few in my life when they were guests here at Spades.

They were the rarest race for us to encounter on earth. They had their own realm. There was beef between them and the Angels, and the Angels operated the supernatural world on earth. So, for the most part, they weren't around.

But, after spending some more time with Laila, I wished they were. Not only because I was dying for a sip of her blood, but because they were fun to be around. Lighthearted. Odd. Funny, yet serious. The way they communicated, the fact that they read our minds every two seconds, their bubbly nature, was amusing. By the end of the day, I was feeling just as safe and at home in her company as Brooke felt with Jeremy.

So how did she solve so many of our problems so quickly? Simple. Or at least, Laila made it seem that way.

From my understanding, this was what Tyler would remember:

A body was found at Spades. I was brought in for an interview, and although he played the bad cop, he knew I didn't do it. He busted my balls a bit, but ultimately concluded that I was telling the truth. While my father had been involved in morally questionable business, he agreed that the apple had fallen far from the tree. That I was a better man than my father had been.

But what about the CI? That, he would have no memory of. It wasn't like when Brooke cast a spell to alter someone's memory. Those perceptions could be altered, the strings could be pulled, as Brooke had said.

No, the only person who could undo what Laila did was another Fae. Or an exceeding powerful Witch. His brain would draw connections where there were none for the bits of information that didn't quite add up. If, at some point, some piece of the puzzle surfaced, like more miles on his car than he thought there were because he drove to Spades this morning, he would somehow rationalize it away, because that was what the human mind wanted to do.

Apparently, according to Laila, our perception of reality was vastly different than reality itself. The brain constantly pushed out the irrelevant information, and that was how Tyler would see any missing pieces from the last few days.

Oh, he left yesterday morning to speak with Brooke at her home and discovered Oliver outside, which led Mason to become his informant? No, no, no. All he remembered was going to Brooke's, but she wasn't home. Then, he got stuck in traffic. That was why it took him so long to get back to the office. It certainly wasn't because he'd confronted a Vampire who revealed the secrets of an underground supernatural bar to him.

"People don't want to believe in things like us," Laila had said. "The power of disbelief is stronger than you might imagine."

And that, I couldn't completely disagree with.

Emory was tasked with getting rid of the footage, then beating the hell out of Mason. He managed that by noon, which was around the same time we sent Tyler on his way.

Sometime around one, Laila said she had to get back to the kids, but that she would send Wyatt and Celena. Or, Rion and Luna, as Brooke remembered them. She gave us all big hugs when she left. And, when she did, I worried less about my jealousy with Brooke and Jeremy. Because when she hugged me, I felt something too.

That sense of community, family, that Brooke seemed to be feeling. There was nothing romantic, certainly nothing sexual, about it. Even if Laila was pleasant enough to look at, it was like when I looked at Ria. While I didn't barf at the sight of her, I cared for her. Which was bizarre, considering I had only met her today, but the fact remained.

When she kissed her husband goodbye, he said, quietly, that he would be home soon. He just wanted to enjoy this for a few moments. Laila expressed her understanding with another kiss and vanished.

Right around that time, Ria landed in the center of the bar with a small suitcase. And Jeremy just watched her. He stood off to the side while I poured us all a drink, watching her.

All, except for Ria. Felt a bit like a slap in the face to pour her one she wouldn't drink.

When I slid the shots of whiskey down the bar, I held one up in the air for Jeremy. "You drink Crown?"

Chuckling, he sat on the edge of the table. "Not anymore, no. Thank you though."

"Are you sure?" Emory asked. "We owe you for this. We owe you big time."

"No, you don't. If anything, you owe my wife." His smile was soft. A bit solemn, but kind. "But don't worry about it. I'm the type of person who can't have one. Or two. Or three. Bottles, not shots."

"Oh." Suddenly, I felt very guilty for offering him even one. "Shit. I'm sorry."

An uncaring wave. "You didn't know. It's not a big deal. Drink. I just can't."

"Really?" Ria asked him. "How long have you been clean?"

Flapping his lips together in a trill, he cocked his head to the side. "Almost three years? My longest stretch was six years. Life kind of blew up a few times, but it's always better when I'm sober. So, I try to stay that way."

"Well, shit," Ria murmured. "Congratulations. Two years, that's huge."

"Almost three." Despite the correction, that smile was an odd combination of solemn and soft. He gave her a once over. "Heroin?"

"How'd you know?" Ria asked.

"Restless legs." He pointed to her foot tapping the floor. "You've run to the bathroom about ten times since we've been here. And you're quiet, which means that's either how you are by nature, or you're irritable and don't want to bite anyone's head off." Ria laughed, and his smile grew a bit more genuine. "And a junkie knows a junkie."

Another laugh, but this one softer. "When do we stop calling ourselves that?"

"Probably when we stop seeing ourselves that way. But it gets easier. Every day when I go to work with my wife, or I'm playing with my kids in the yard, or anything else that distracts me from wanting a needle. Every day gets a little bit easier."

"Until you relapse?"

"Well, once upon a time, I was clean for a couple hundred thousand years." He shrugged. "I'm trying to beat that record this time around."

Her face screwed up. So did everyone else's in the room.

"Like I said," Jeremy said, "we'll all catch up eventually. Too much information to process in a night. For now, celebrate. I'm just gonna sit here and think about a time when Drogo didn't hate me for hugging his girlfriend."

I snorted, giving a half smile. "I don't hate you."

"No, you're just a little worried. And I get it." Holding his hands up at his sides in surrender, he returned my smirk. "I was hesitant, too, when I learned about all this. I didn't always remember, you know. Laila, she saw more of the story than I did when it started, and even that messed with me. But soon, you'll remember how good of friends we were."

"I'm looking forward to it," I said.

And I was.

I was looking forward to everything. Everything that came next.

Ria, getting clean. Brooke, and the new version of herself she would become as she remembered who she once was. Getting to know the man that I had once called a brother, or cousin, or whatever it was that we referred to ourselves as. Learning about a life that I lived apparently hundreds of thousands of years ago. Seeing the way that it changed me, the way that it changed Brooke, and maybe even the way that it would change my best friend.

After he took a shot, he stood and asked Ria, "So you've got restless legs, huh?"

"That'd be why I'm standing," she said.

With a big smile, Emory walked to the jukebox in the corner, popped in a quarter, and gave her the biggest smile. He wasn't much of a smiler, but with her, he reminded me of the kid he was before life came for him full throttle. "Well, come on. Let's get moving then."

Ria laughed. "Fuck off."

He didn't. Still smiling, he took her hand, brought her to the open floor near the pool table, and got her dancing. She laughed some more, and so did he, and they swayed, and twirled, and it was a nice sight to behold.

And that, I was excited to witness as well. What came next for them.

Was also excited to see what Jeremy thought of it, considering my theory, but I could hardly call his expression a smile when I looked that way. It was, by technicality, a smile, but there was a certain grief in his eyes that I had a hard time understanding.

But I wasn't one to beat around the bush. "Are they what I think they are?"

Jeremy turned my way. Pressing his lips together, he shrugged again. "Their story's a bit more complicated."

Barely loud enough to be heard over the jukebox, Brooke whispered, "Wait. Are you saying that Ria and Emory are paired souls too?"

Jeremy closed the distance between the table he'd been standing at and leaned over the bar where Brooke sat. "Are you two still good at keeping secrets?"

"We covered up a murder today. What do you think?" Brooke asked.

Glancing at Ria and Emory over his shoulder, Jeremy lowered his voice. "They were. But it wasn't just the two of them. There were two others. Two men, and the four of them lived happily ever after. Until we all died, but that's a whole other thing."

Well, hadn't seen that one coming.

AFTERWORD

A note from the author

As always, thanks so much for reading! I hope you liked it! But...

Well, I think a lot of you guys started reading my books because you like the blunt nature of mine you see on Tiktok, so I'm just gonna say it. I'm not all that confident about this book. While writing it, I was going through a really rough divorce, still learning the ropes of dictation since nerve damage and chronic pain in my arms has kept me from typing, and —on top of it all—was sick with Covid while going over my final edits.

I'm hoping it's more imposture syndrome than quality of the writing itself, but suffice it to say, I wish I would've had more bandwidth than I did while writing this one. But a deadline's a deadline! Promise, the next one will be better. Please don't give up on reading my work if this one doesn't fulfill your usual expectations for me!

And, if you *didn't* hate it, and you're wondering where the pre-order is for book 3, you might wanna follow my socials for more info on that. Brooke and Declan's story isn't over, but I think Emory's and Ria's might come first. (And yup, for those of you who've read Origins, I mean, Sanvi's, Eike's, Volke's, and Errol's.)

Raven's Dawn is next up, and then Eluding Destiny Book 15. I'd like to release a book in both of those series this year and possibly start Ria's series by the end of 2024.

I can't say much of anything for certain, though, because life has been too chaotic lately, and I don't want to get crushed under another deadline. My other pen name (C.R. Gray, for mystery/thriller/suspense) has also been taking up a lot of my time lately.

But there's definitely more coming. I just don't wanna give you a date and then release a book I know could be better because I'm rushing to meet a deadline.

Thanks again for reading, and for your understanding <3

Much love,
    Charlie

ABOUT THE AUTHOR

Charlie is a... Okay, talking about myself in third person is weird.

Nice to meet you! My name's Charlie Nottingham, and my whole world revolves around fantasy. When I'm not writing a new book, I'm either hanging out with my dogs, talking with my fans online, or reading some amazing urban fantasy, paranormal romance, or fantasy romance series (always a series, never a stand-alone, because I hate to fall for a character and never see them again). Or re-watching some Buffy or Supernatural. (They never get old!)

www.ingramcontent.com/pod-product-compliance
Lightning Source LLC
Chambersburg PA
CBHW071133200626
46817CB00018B/2938